Black Scarface II

The Rise of An American Kingpin

A Novel By
Jimmy DaSaint & Freeway Rick Ross

Acknowledgements from Jimmy DaSaint

First and foremost I give all my praise to God, my strength, soul and savior. I would like to give a big thanks to my co-writer Freeway Rick Ross.

Also I'd like to thank the following list of people: my mother, Belinda, my sisters, Dawn, Tammy and Tanya. My brother Sean. To my two sons-Marquise and Niguel. Thanks to all my good friends for their support and encouragement. It means a lot to me just knowing you have my back.

Wallace "Duke" Gray, and the entire Gray. Robert Hennigan, Sekue Clark, Duran-Norfleet, Kenneth "Cheese" Johnson, and my entire ICH family-Colossus, Reese, Sport, Bossman, Scarfo, A-Town, Shorty-Raw, HH-Spady, Var, T. P. Dollarz, and Young Savage.

To my fans, you truly are a blessing and I thank you for your continued support. I write for you.

To all the bookstores and vendors, thank you for keeping your shelves filled with my novels. Empire Books, DC Book Diva, Black & Nobel, Street Knowledge Books, Amaiya Ent., Expressions, Divin Books In the Hood, and Xanyell and Quada, from Horizon Books; thanks for holding me down always.

To all the men and woman incarcerated in the State and Federal prison across the county, I'd like to say thank you for all your support and uplifting letters. Stay positive in your moment of darkness, as the light always shines on those who believe.

R.I. P to Man, Mark, Troy, Rob and Harold "Georgie" Johnson.

Jimmy DaSaint

Acknowledgements
from
Freeway Rick Ross

First I would like to thank my mother, Annie May Ross-McGee, for showing strength and support through the dark times in my life. You never left my side for one moment.

To my seven beautiful future kings and queens, always remember your father loves you more than anything in this world: Tommy, Vick, Rick, Carrie, Rickeya, Kardo and Jamal. I also would like to give a shout out to their beautiful mothers.

To all my brothers and sisters that's doing time under these unjust laws-be strong and never give up. Keep your heads to the sky!

To all my fallen comrades, may y'all rest in peace and know that you'll never be forgotten. To all my brothers and sisters that are out committing senseless crimes-Wake Up!

A very special shout-out to all my fans and supporters who have and continue to write and support me. Thanks for visiting my website www.freewayenterprise.com , I truly thank you.

If there is anyone who may feel left out, don't. You are always thought of and acknowledged within me.

Freeway Rick Ross

A RIGHTEOUS MAN MAY HAVE MANY TROUBLES
BUT THE LORD WILL DELIVER HIM FROM THEM ALL
PSALMS 34:19

BLACK SCARFACE II –THE RISE OF AN AMERICAN KINGPIN

BLACK SCARFACE II

Published by:
DASAINT ENTERTINAMENT
Po Box 97
Bala Cynwyd, PA 19004

Website: www.dasatinentertainment.com
Edited by a very talented woman and my dear friend-Panzie R.

PROLOGUE

Ardmore, Pennsylvania, a small town right outside of Philadelphia...

Face, Reese and Doc all climbed inside the tinted black Lexus. The two suitcases filled with money were lying on the back seat. As Reese pulled his car back onto the road, Face sat in the passenger seat with his arms folded across his chest. His eyes were closed but his mind raced with thoughts.

While Reese drove back to Philly, feelings of relief and satisfaction roamed throughout Face's body. He had just killed and robbed his number one enemy; Hood. The same

man who murdered his father, Norman, and beat up and raped his mother, Pamela.

While inside the house, Reese, his best friend since childhood, shot and killed Hood's wife Britney. The only lives that were spared in the house had been their own and Hood's scared young children, Robbie and Arianna.

The reason Face didn't kill them along with their parents was because Arianna was an innocent little girl and Robbie was his younger brother. And since they had both been tied up, blindfolded and gagged, neither one of them knew who the killers were.

Face sat back thinking about the good, bad and ugliness of his young life. At 19 years old he had lived a fast and violent life. Face had seen it all, from mayhem and drugs to murder.

So had his partner and best friend, Reese. Although they were totally opposite, they both possessed total love, respect and loyalty towards the other.

Images of faces flashed inside Face's head. They were of his loving and overprotective mother, Pamela, Tasha, his beautiful young girlfriend, Veronica, Pamela's best friend and the woman who had taken his virginity when he was twelve years old, Momma, his surrogate Grandmother that he loved with all his heart, and D.J., his close friend and Reese's younger brother. Face also imagined Jay. Jay was his mother's boyfriend who had been brutally shot 19 times by Hood's men and was now paralyzed from the waist down and confined to a wheelchair for the rest of his life.

In the car filled with complete silence images of others continued to flash inside Face's head. Gloria, his attractive sex partner, that moved back to New York to finish her law degree. She had moved to get away from Face, the man she had fallen deeply in love with, but could never have for her very own. Truck, his good friend and former drug boss, that was now serving a 25 year Federal prison sentence after getting set up by his nephew, A-Rock, in an FBI undercover drug sting. Quincy, his close friend from Los Angeles, California, whom he loved like an older brother. Face couldn't wait for Quincy to get out of prison, come to Philly, and join his crew.

When the image of Killa-D appeared, Face smiled. He and Reese had both enjoyed shooting and killing Hood's top street enforcer. Thanks to Passion, Reese's attractive stripper girlfriend, killing Killa-D was a lot easier than they had originally expected. His death had been long overdue, and with all the information Killa-D told them about Hood's drug operation, it was well worth it. The final image that appeared in Face's mind was of the crooked cop, Ron Perry. He was another one of Hood's loyal soldiers that Face couldn't wait to one day kill.

When Face finally opened his eyes, they were back in Philly, driving down Walnut Street. Face turned around and looked at his strange white friend, Doc. He glanced at the large black bag Doc was holding on his lap, and smiled. Inside the bag was a large glass jar that contained Hood's freshly removed heart. Watching Doc surgically open Hood's chest and remove his heart was the ultimate revenge. Deep down in his soul Face knew that it was just the beginning. Now, the legacy of the man who would become known as 'BLACK SCAR-FACE' had begun…

CHAPTER 69

Two days later...

The news about the violent murders of Hood and his wife that took place in their Ardmore, PA home had spread throughout the city. People in barbershops, hair salons, neighborhood bars and pool halls were all talking about it.

As for Hood's crew, it was quickly disintegrating; the 'Big Boss' was now dead and Killa-D, the top lieutenant in Hood's crew was nowhere to be found. Without its two leaders, Hood's

drug organization was in complete chaos.

Inside the FBI building...

Agent McDonald paced back and forth across the room holding a rolled up copy of the Philadelphia Daily Newspaper. His partner, Agent Powaski looked on as he sipped his coffee while McDonald vented frustration.

"What the hell is going on! I can't believe it, Steve! As soon as the boss gives us the okay to start a new investigation on Hood and his crew, the son-of-a-bitch gets murdered inside

his own house! And whoever did it took his fucking heart out!"

"He must have really pissed somebody off " Agent Powaski calmly replied as he took another sip of coffee.

"We can’t seem to catch a break! In the last seven months we have lost two of our informants! And now this!" Agent McDonald walked over to his partner and unrolled the newspaper.

"Look at this Steve!" he said showing him the front page headline. "PHILLY DRUG BOSS SLAIN INSIDE HIS HOUSE!" "Somebody robbed us of getting revenge on Hood!

And now they're gonna pay!" McDonald stated seriously.

"But, we ain't got a clue who did it. The investigators said the job was spotless! No prints, clues, or suspects! Nothing!" Powaski replied. "Maybe it was an inside job," he added.

"I thought about that, but Hood had a very tight circle around him," McDonald said thoughtfully. "He had that no good Philly cop, his body guard, Big-C and his right hand man, Killa-D."

"Maybe Killa-D is behind it. He ain't been seen around since Hood's murder," Powaski said.

For a moment McDonald considered the idea, then said, "No, I doubt it. Killa-D would never cross Hood."

Powaski stood up from his chair and said, "Well partner, one boss is down and we'll see who rises to the top to take his place. When that happens, that will tell us everything we need to know."

South Philly...

On the corner of 23rd and Tasker, Ron Perry pulled up and parked his black Chevy Tahoe. A large heavyset black man, standing around six feet, eight inches tall, quickly walked over and got inside. They shook hands, then Ron Perry slowly pulled off and drove down the street.

The big man's name was Big C and he had been Hood's number one bodyguard. In fact it had been Big C who discovered Hood and Britney's dead bodies and their children who were bound, gagged, blindfolded and terrified. Detectives had questioned him, then let him go, because they couldn't conclusively finger him in the murders. But, to the police, he was still a suspect. Robbie and Arianna were taken downtown to Child Protective Services. Later Britney's parents arrived and gained temporary custody of them while the adoption proceedings were pending.

"Where the fuck is Killa-D?" Ron Perry asked Big C, as they drove down 23rd street.

"I been callin' him for the past two days," Big C replied, looking wide eyed and gravely concerned.

"He ain't call me back. It's like he disappeared from the face of the earth!"

Ron Perry looked over at Big C and said, "We gotta find out who did this!"

"I been on it Ron, but nobody don't know a thing. Hood kept his circle tight and small. It was only you, me, Killa-D, and Hood. And I was just the body guard. My job was to check

up on him every morning and keep an eye on his children."

"So, you didn't see anything strange at all on your way over to Hood's house?" Ron Perry asked, as he turned his truck down Broad Street.

Big C sat back pondering the question for a moment.

" You know what? Now that you mention it I did see a strange black car pass me as I was headed for the house."

"Do you remember what type of car it was?" Ron Perry asked. "Not really. It was still kind of dark. But, if I had to guess, I would say it was either a Lexus or an Acura Legend...Until now it had completely slipped my mind."

"Did you see how many people were inside?"

"No, I remember the windows being tinted," Big C said.

Ron Perry shook his head and said, "Maybe the people inside were responsible for killing Hood and Britney."

"Maybe. Or it could have been just someone rushing off to work" Big C replied.

Inside Pamela's living room…

She was sitting on the sofa with Face. Reese had just dropped Face off and told him he would be back in an hour to pick him up. Pamela was dressed and ready to go to work. But, whenever Face came to see her, she would stop whatever she was doing and give him her undivided attention.

Face reached over and grabbed Pamela's hands, then he stared straight into her eyes and whispered, "Mom, I got him."

Pamela looked at Face's excited expression and smiled. She didn't have to ask any questions. She already knew what he meant. Tears welled up in her eyes and started falling down the sides of her face. "I...I...seen...it on...the news!" she cried.

Face reached out and gave his mother a long warm hug. "I did it for you Mom. For you and Jay. And my father," he whispered into her ear.

"Thank you, Baby. Thank you so much," Pamela said, finally feeling some relief inside her grieving soul.

"Where's Jay?" Face asked. "I have a surprised for him."

"He's upstairs in the bedroom," Pamela replied sadly.

"What's wrong?" Face asked noticing the sad expression on her face.

"Jay has gotten a lot worse since he came home from the hospital. All he talks about is dying, and it's starting to get to me. I've been doing everything I can to make him happy but he won't let me" she replied, wiping her tears away with the back of her hands. "Face, it's really starting to stress me out. "

Face reached out and hugged his mother again. "Don't worry Mom, everything will be all right."

Face hated to see his mother in pain or crying. She was the most important person in his life and seeing her hurting had always taken a toll on him.

"Mom, you go ahead to work. I'll go and talk with Jay," Face said, as they stood up from the sofa.

"So, is Jay's surprise inside that backpack?" Pamela asked, pointing to the bag that was strapped around Face's shoulder.

"Yeah," he smiled.

"Well, good luck. 'Cause I ain't been able to make him smile once," she said as they walked over to the front door.

After Face walked Pamela to her car, they kissed and hugged before she got inside and drove off. When Face walked back into the house, he headed up the stairs with a smirk on

his face. He couldn't wait to show Jay his big surprise.

Southwest Philly...

Pamela pulled over and parked her car on the corner of 53rd and Chester Avenue. She just sat there letting tears stream down her face. The news of Hood's death had finally brought

her the relief she longed for so many years. A part of her still couldn't believe that the monster was actually dead; the man who was responsible for most of her pain.

After a brief moment, Pamela smiled, started her car and drove off. She was headed to her job; working at Tasha's new and successful real estate company.

Lewisburg federal prison...

Truck laid aside the Philadelphia Newspaper after reading the entire story of the savage murders of Hood and his wife. There was no one that he hated more. With a smile across his face

he thought about Face, wondering if his young friend had anything to do with killing Hood. Truck knew that Face also felt hatred towards Hood, but he had no idea how deep that hatred

actually went. Since coming to prison, Truck had wanted for nothing. Face had kept his word and made sure Truck was straight. Every single month Tasha would send Truck a money order and several new books to read.

Truck was one of several names on a list that Face had given Tasha. The list contained friends of Face's who were doing time, either in federal or state prison. And Face wanted to make sure they were all well taken care of.

Back at Pamela's...

When Face walked into the bedroom, Jay was sitting in his wheelchair, staring down at his legs.

"What's up, Jay?" Face said, waking him from his daze. Jay looked up and tried to muster a smile.

"What's up, Face?" he said solemnly.

Face smiled and said, "I got something for you," taking the back pack off his shoulder.

"Is it a gun?" Jay joked. But a part of him hoped it was.

"No, I came to bring you this," Face said unzipping the back pack and reaching his hand down inside.

When Face pulled out the large glass jar containing Hood's recently removed heart, Jay surprisingly stated, "What the hell is that?"

Face brought the jar closer and said, "this is Hood's heart! I promised you that I would get it for you... remember?"

Jay reached out and grabbed the jar from Face's hands. He slowly turned it around inspecting the heart from every angle. It was the strangest thing he had ever seen. "You, you...really...did it!" Jay exclaimed, staring raptly at the heart. "I can't...I can't believe it," he continued awestruck.

"Well believe it, Jay. Hood is dead and that's the man's heart you're holding." Face said.

After staring at the jar, Jay sat it down in his lap and said, "Face, I need you to wheel me into the bathroom."

Face walked behind his wheelchair and started to roll Jay out of the bedroom. When they entered the bathroom Face rolled him over to the toilet. He watched as Jay unscrewed the jar and took the lid off.

A foul pungent stench permeated the room almost instantly. Jay quickly dumped the heart into the toilet, and replaced the lid on the jar.

"Fuck Hood!" he said, then hit the flush handle and watched the heart flush away.

When Jay's two nurses came by the house to check up on him Face was walking out the front door. Before he climbed into Reese's car he looked up at the bedroom window and noticed Jay staring out at him. They waved good-bye to each other, then Face got inside the car.

When Reese pulled off, Jay sat back in his wheelchair. He was happy that Hood was finally dead, but Jay still had a lot of personal problems to overcome.

CHAPTER 70

A few hours later...

Ron Perry couldn't believe it. He had just learned that Killa-D's body had just been found out in Fairmount Park. And the black Mercedes Benz that was registered in his name was parked a few feet away from his burnt corpse. Ron Perry sat inside his truck trying his best to hold back his tears. Big C didn't want to look in his eyes. He could only imagine what he was going through. His two partners were both dead and they didn't have a single suspect. Hood had so many enemies, that he didn't know where to start looking.

"Did Killa-D say anything to y'all the last time y'all talked?" Ron Perry asked as he closed his cell phone and put it inside his jacket pocket.

After a long sigh, Big C looked over at Ron Perry and said, "He asked me if I wanted to go to the strip clubs with him."

"The strip club? Hood told him to stay away from the strip clubs for a while!" Ron Perry said angrily.

"I know and I told Killa that he shouldn't go. But, I believe he went anyway."

"Damn!" Ron said banging his fist down on the steering wheel. "He knew better! Do you know what club he went to?"

"Probably the Ultimate Fantasy. He's been trying to get with that girl that works there. That thick pretty one that he ain't have sex with."

Ron Perry sat back in deep thought.

"What chu thinking about?" Big C curiously asked.

"Something here ain't right. It's not adding up and Im'a get to the bottom of this!"

Big C watched as Ron Perry started his truck and drove down the street. He sat back watching Ron mumble some words under his breath. When Ron Perry stopped his truck at a red light he looked over at Big C and said, “somebody’s gonna pay severely for fucking up my meal ticket!” Big C saw the sincerity in Ron’s eyes and just nodded his head in agreement.

Outside the Denrich Apartments building...

Face and Reese had just placed two large suitcases into the trunk of the car. When they got back inside the car Reese looked at Face and asked, "So, where to now?"

"Face gave Reese a sly smile and said, "We're going to Jersey."

"For what?" Reese asked as he pulled off and drove down the street.

"To meet the Gomez brothers and give them back their money, " Face said with all importance.

"What? Face are you crazy? Did Doc slip something in your drink?" Reese shouted out.

"No, Reese just listen to me."

"I'm all ears," Reese said as he continued to drive.

“Killa-D told us that the Gomez brothers were Hood's drug connect. Hood and Killa-D was supposed to meet them today at 3:00 o'clock. We need a connect, Reese. Now, what better way to get one than to take them their money that someone else owes them? I know it sounds crazy, Reese. But just trust me. One thing I found out about drug dealers is that money always comes first. Nothing else matters." Face said.

"But the Gomez brothers are Hood's friends. They will kill us on the spot!" Reese replied. "Hood made those guys millions. Maybe even billions. Going to see them is like signing

your own death certificate!"

"Maybe not. Didn't Killa-D say something about Hood and the Gomez brothers not getting along lately?"

"Yeah, but so what? It could be anything," Reese replied as he cruised his car onto the expressway traffic.

"You're right, but something is telling me, Reese, that it's more than that. And the only way to find out is to go see for ourselves. I know it sounds foolish, but just trust me Reese. Everything is gonna turn out right," Face said confidently.

Reese glanced over and said, "But, if you're wrong, we're both dead men!"

"But, if my intuitions are right, we'll finally get the connect we need that will make us both rich," Face said with a grin.

"You're taking a big chance, Face. We don't know nothing about the Gomez brothers. Nothing!"

Face looked across at Reese and said, "Do you know what Mouse used to tell me?"

"What?" Reese asked.

"He used to tell me that chances make champions. That the difference between men of power and wealth and men of poverty are the chances they take and the choices they make. Reese, I'm willing to take this chance," Face replied.

After a long sigh Reese looked over at Face and smiled. "Fuck it," he said. "We only live once!", then he turned up the volume on his new Ruff Ryders CD.

Cherry Hill, New Jersey,-Forty five minutes later…

Reese pulled up in front of a beautiful white home, then he and Face both nervously got out of the car and looked around.

"This is the address that Killa-D gave us," Face said.

"What if he was lying to us?"

"Well, there's only one way to find out," Face said as he walked up to the front door and slammed the ornate lion head door knocker onto the brass knocker plate, then stepped

back and waited.

Moments later a big Spanish looking man with an intense expression opened the front door and asked, "Yeah, how can I help you?"

"We're here to see the Gomes brothers," Face told him.

"And who are you?" the man curiously asked.

"I'm Face and this is my friend Reese," he answered.

"And what business do you have with the Gomez brothers?"

the big Spaniard said.

"We're here to talk business and bring them something," Face replied.

"And what is that Senor?"

"Look, we don't have all day. Either you tell'em two guys are out here that they really needs to meet with or we'll just take the money and come back some other time," Face said.

"Money? What money, Senor?"

"Their money. Now, can we see them or not?"

"One moment Senor, I will see if they will meet with you," the man said, then closed the door.

"Face, you crazy man! You can't talk to them people like that! You sure Doc ain't put something in those sleeping pills?" Reese exclaimed.

Before Face could respond the front door swung open and the big Spanish man said,

"Señors, please come in. The Gomez brothers will meet with you. They are most curious about the money you say belongs to them. Please, right this way, Señors."

As they stepped through the front door, they immediately saw two more big Spanish men standing around as if they were expecting trouble at any moment.

The Spanish man closed the door behind them, then immediately began patting Face and Reese down, checking for weapons. Luckily, they had left their .9s and cell phone in the car. Something Face had suggested while on their way to the house. "Follow me, please," the man said politely after not finding any weapons.

Face and Reese followed the big Spanish man down a flight of stairs that led to the basement. The two other Spanish looking men stayed close behind them. When they entered the basement they saw two other Spanish men who were significantly smaller than the guards that let them in the house. These two Spaniards were sitting on the sofa watching a big screen TV in a well laid out room. There was a large pool table, a built in bar, and a state of the art stereo system that was all nestled on plush white carpet.

"They are both clean, Senors," the big Spaniard told his bosses in Spanish, then he turned away, walked to the bar and took a seat on one of the bar stools. The big guy folded his arms across his massive chest and stared closely at them. 'If they are not cops, then they are two very foolish men', he thought to himself.

"So, how can we help you two men?" Rico Gomez asked.

"You can help us a lot. And I believe me and my partner can help y'all a lot, also," Face said.

Rico laughed and said, "And how is that?"

Face looked into Rico's eyes. His face was as stern as it had ever been. "We're looking for a major connect!"

Rico and Jose both started laughing. "Either y'all two men are crazy or you have balls the size of melons," Rico said.

"What makes you think that you and your friend can just come up here and ask for a connect? My friend we don't even know y'all. Y'all could be cops, or worse, federal agents or informants!" he added.

Then Face said, "Mr. I ain't no cop or no informant. Killa-D told me all about you right before I killed him."

Rico and Jose both stopped laughing, "Killa-D is dead?" Jose asked surprisingly.

"Yeah, and so is Hood," Reese said.

"Who killed Hood?" Rico asked.

"I did. I shot him right between the eyes. Right after I cut out his heart," Face said .

"I'm sure y'all have heard about it by now."

Rico and Jose both stood up from the sofa. They couldn't believe what they just heard.

"Hood was a good friend. He made us a lot of money," Rico said.

"We could make you a lot more," Face confidently replied.

"How old are you?" Jose asked.

"We're both nineteen," Face answered.

He stood back nodding his head, knowingly. "Young lions, huh?"

"Young starving lions," Face corrected.

"You killed a major asset for us. What if I have my men shoot you both full of holes for what you have done to my friend?" Rico said.

"Then you won't have nobody in the city to take Hood's place. We ain't here for no trouble, Sir. We just here to make money. And to bring y'all back your money," Face said.

"And what money is that?" Rico asked.

"The three million dollars that Hood owed you before he died!" Face answered.

"You have it?"

Yeah, we have two large suitcases in the trunk of our car. Each one has a million and a half inside. That's why we're here, to bring y'all back your money," Face told them.

The two brothers began speaking rapidly in Spanish. Neither Face or Reese understood a single word they said.

"Why didn't y'all just keep the money?" Rico said.

Face looked deep into Rico's eyes and said, "Because we ain't no thieves. We're hustlers! And any money we get we want to earn it." Then, he reached into Reese's jacket pocket,

took out the car keys, and tossed them to the big Spanish guy sitting at the bar. "Y'all money is in the trunk. We have no use for it," he said.

Jose nodded his head and the big Spanish guy jumped off the bar stool and rushed up the stairs. They stood around eyeing each other until the big Spaniard came back down the

stairs carrying the two suitcases. He sat them down near Jose's feet. "The money is inside like he said," the guy told him.

Jose and Rico walked near the bar to talk amongst themselves. Face and Reese stood watching them the entire time.

"Whatchu think, Face?"

"Just be cool, Reese. We'll find out in a minute," Face replied.

When the two brothers walked back over to them Rico said, "We have to check you out. We want to make sure everything is fine before we make our decision."

"No problem. We can come back in a few days", Face said.

Rico laughed and said, "No my young friend it don't work that way. You two will stay here with us as our guests until we find out everything we need to know about y'all two. If everything turns out alright, then we can do some business."

"And what if it don't?" Reese asked.

"Then both of y'all will die the same way Hood did. With a bullet between your eyes and your hearts ripped from your chest," Jose responded.

"Y'all will both know everything in a few days. So get comfortable," Jose told them.

When Rico nodded his head, their men quickly pulled out their loaded weapons. "Mira ellos, hasta nos volvemos," Rico said in Spanish; (watch them until we get back), he said, before

he and Jose grabbed the two suitcases, walked over to the stairs, and out of the basement.

CHAPTER 71

Later that night...

Ron Perry walked out of the Ultimate Fantasy Gentlemen's Club with all the information he needed. In less than one hour he found out that not only had Killa-D been in the club on the night he disappeared, but when he left a woman known as Passion had been with him. "The two hundred dollars I paid for this information was well worth it", he thought.

When Ron Perry climbed back into his truck, Big C was patiently waiting inside for him.

"Did you find out anything?" he asked, turning the volume down on the radio.

"Yeah, I found out a whole lot more than what I came for. Them bitches will sell their soul for a few dollars," he said as they both laughed.

"So, what chu find?"

"Killa-D was there on the night he disappeared and he left with a woman named Passion. The same woman he had been trying to fuck for God knows how long. I also found out that Passion's boyfriend is some street thug named Reese. I also found out that Reese is the driver of a black Lexus."

"Reese!" Bid C shouted.

"You know him?"

"Yeah, I know his bitch ass! I know all about him," Big C said angrily.

"That girl inside told me that Passion loves the ground Reese walks on," Ron Perry said as he pulled off and drove down the street.

"Then why would she leave with Killa-D?" Big C asked confusedly.

Ron Perry looked over at Big C and said, "It was a common set up. I've seen so many of them, just like this one. Passion set up Killa-D for Reese; the man she loves."

"That no good bitch!" Big C said.

"Don't worry Big C, Passion and her man, Reese, are gonna pay for what they did to Killa-D. And so will all their loved ones," Ron Perry said with an evil grin.

Inside the Lincoln Green Apartments...

Passion was sitting inside her apartment waiting for Reese to call her back. She had been calling him all day long and her intuition told her that something was wrong. Passion left over twenty five messages on his voice mail and she even called Face's cell but was unable to reach him as well.

When the phone rang she quickly answered, "Hello?" hoping it was Reese.

"Passion what's up? It's me, White Chocolate," her girlfriend said.

"What's up White Chocolate?"

"I had to call you and tell you something really important."

"What is it?" Passion asked, hearing the seriousness in her voice.

"Some guy came by the club tonight asking a lot of questions About you. I think he was a cop."

"What?" Passion said. "Did you tell him anything?" she asked.

"No, I wasn't feeling his vibe, so I stepped off. But, I saw him talking to a few of the other girls," White Chocolate replied.

"Did you see what he was driving?" Passion asked.

"Yeah, I saw when he left out the club. He got inside a black Yukon with some big guy in the passenger seat."

"Shit!" Passion said.

"Is everything alright, Passion?"

"Yeah, everything is fine," she lied.

"You know if you ever need me girl, I'm here for you," White Chocolate said with all sincerity. "It would kill me if I lost another close friend," she added.

"Don't worry White Chocolate, I'ma be fine but thanks anyway," Passion said.

"So will you be here tomorrow night?"

"No, I'm gonna take some time off," Passion said.

"Well you be safe girl. I'll call you if I find out anything else. "

After they both hung up the phone, Passion sat back with a worried look on her face. She tried to call Reese again, but only got his voice mail.

"Reese, where the hell are you?" she asked out loud to the empty room as her eyes filled with tears. As she sat back on the sofa her tears fell down her cheeks. With fear resting in her soul, all she could do was sit and wait.

Inside Face's apartment...

Tasha knew that something had to be terribly wrong when Face didn't call her back. She left over thirty messages on his voice mail. Her mind was racing with thoughts and she was more scared than she had ever been in her life. Every passing minute brought more fear. She wanted to tell Face her good news; their real estate company had just purchased two commercial properties in Center City, but Face had not answered his phone or responded to her voice mails.

As she paced back and forth across the living room floor the tears fell down her concerned face. She looked at the clock on the wall and noted the time. It was 1:49 P.M., three hours past the time Face was usually at home.

* * *

The big black truck pulled up right across the street from Momma's house and parked.

"That's where Reese grew up at. His grandmother and lil' brother still live there," Big C said as he pointed to the small row house. Ron Perry nodded his head with an wicked look on his

face.

"In due time," he said as he slowly pulled off and drove down the dark street.

* * *

Rico and Jose Gomez sat inside their limousine sipping champagne. The low sound of salsa music came from the speakers. Rico had just hung up the phone, after talking to one of his many sources who lived and worked in the Philadelphia area.

"So far our two young friends are clean," he said with a smile.

"Hopefully, it stays that way," Jose replied as he took a sip of champagne.

"I have to admit, the two young men have a lot of heart," Rico said.

"Yeah, and ambition also. The one called Face reminds me a lot of Hood…the way Hood was when we first met him" Jose replied.

"Jose, I think you're wrong this time. That kid, Face, is a lot hungrier. I can see it in his eyes. He's a born leader. It's all in his attitude," Rico stated.

"You sound like you like the kid."

"There's something about him, I must admit. He's totally different from anyone that I've ever met before, especially for his age. It's like the kid has an old soul," Rico replied.

"Don't forget, Rico, they killed Hood and Killa-D. And right now our money in Philadelphia is froze," Jose said as he sat his glass down.

"Hood and Killa-D were both good friends. But, they are gone now. And someone younger and more hungry has replaced them. What the two men did was total validation, but at the same time Jose, business is business and friends come and go."

"So, if all turns out well, you're willing to work with them?" Jose asked.

"Maybe it won't be a bad idea. Since Hood is no longer around we're gonna need someone to take his place now. So why not the man who killed him?" Rico said with a grin.

"But, we don't know if Face can be trusted or not. Will he stay loyal if the pressure ever comes his way? At least Hood was loyal to us."

"I don't know why, Jose, but something keeps telling me that Face, is one of a kind. Just what he did today says a lot about him. He had heart. He's hungry and the kid is ambitious."

"That's a scary combination," Rico said in a somber tone. "And don't forget he ain't afraid to kill," he added.

"Well, let's not jump to conclusions so fast Rico. We still got some more checking up to do on Face and his friend, Reese. Tomorrow we should know everything we need to know about them." Jose said as he reached over and turned up the volume on the radio.

As the two brothers sat back enjoying the comfortable ride, the sounds of salsa music filled the limousine. Moments later their limousine pulled up in front of the Rittenhouse Hotel, where two beautiful white women were waiting inside the lobby.

Cherry Hill, New Jersey...

Face and Reese sat on the sofa and watched as the two large Spanish guards were replaced with two more Spanish men, equal to their size and strength. For almost twelve hours they had been sitting around talking and watching the large screen TV. Every so often one of them stood up and went to use the small bathroom down the hall. Each time one of the large Spanish men would follow close behind them, then return with them, his .9mm pistol clutched tightly in one hand.

Reese looked over at Face and whispered, "Face, I don't think this was a good idea, man. What if the Gomez brothers find out some bad shit about us?"

"Reese, everything is cool man. We ain't got nothing to hide. And the only bad news they gonna find is the bad news we done told them; the news about killing Hood and Killa-D,"

Face said in a low tone.

"You don't think that will hurt us?" Reese asked.

"I don't think so Reese. If so they would have shot us. These people don't play around, Reese. They all about business. And their business is all about making money. And lots of it."

"So, you don't think they're upset about what happened to Hood and Killa-D?"

"I'm sure they are. Hood made these guys millions. But the reality is, Hood is dead and they need someone to take his place. Killa-D told us that the Gomez brothers are two of the biggest drug dealers in the entire world. If that's true then we are gonna blow up big time. This is what we've always wanted, Reese," Face said excitedly.

"You ain't afraid, Face?" Reese asked looking deep into eyes.

"Reese, people pray every day to one day go to a better place. But, when it's time for them to go, they begin to get afraid. Scared. Reese, I'm not afraid to die. And I'm not

afraid of power. The only thing I'm afraid of is failure", Face said. "Failure scares me worse than death."

Reese grinned and said, Well, we in this mess together. If I gotta die, I'm glad it's with you."

Face reached over and touched his shoulder. After a long sigh he said, "Reese, ain't nobody gonna die. This is how these things work. Some men die or go to prison and just as quickly another man steps up to take his place. We ain't gonna die. We ain't even started living, yet! Just trust me, everything is gonna turn out all right."

* * *

Veronica laid in her bed alone watching one of her many home-made sex tapes on TV. She had copies of all of her secretly made sex tapes transferred onto small discs. Whenever she had free time she would lay back and enjoy watching one of her sexual episodes. Her long list of powerful, wealthy white clients included lawyers, doctors, corporate businessmen, police officers, and even two judges. Veronica had enough raw sexual footage on them that would start a large scale public scandal, and rock the city on its very foundation if anyone ever found out. That's why only two other people knew about her sex tapes; her best friend's Pamela and Face.

Throughout Philadelphia's most prestigious and elite, Veronica was known as 'the mistress for the wealthy- The rich man's whore'. Her reputation as a high-class escort was well known and whispered about among influential people. They paid top dollar for her to make their dreams and wishes a reality, and she never disappointed them.

After the tape ended she replaced it with another one. In the tranquility of her cozy bedroom she laid back across the bed. Her naked brown body sank into the silk sheets as she watched herself on the TV screen. She placed her hand between her legs, put two fingers inside her warm wetness and closed her eyes.

CHAPTER 72

Two days later...

When the Gomez brothers walked into the basement, Face and Reese quickly stood up from the sofa. For two long days both of them had been nervously waiting to hear the decision that could change or end their lives. The two brothers walked up to them and everyone was very serious. Four armed bodyguards surrounded Face and Reese. Rico stood directly in front of Face. Neither man blinked an eye. Then he extended his hand, and said, "Mr. Norman 'Face' Smith, Jr. and Mr. Maurice Daniels welcome to the family!" They all shook hands and hugged. Face and Reese both passed the test and now they were the newest and youngest members of the notorious Nicaraguan, Gomez drug cartel. They were both relieved and the excitement of the moment ran throughout their bodies.

Jose was carrying a small black briefcase. He opened it and took out two new cell phones and a white piece of paper, "Here, these are for y'all. The new numbers and everything else y'all will need is on this paper," he said, handing them the phones and the paper. Face took the piece of paper and the cell phone from his hand and looked it over. The name Roberto Chevez was written with a number beside it and more information was written just below it.

"My friend Roberto will be the man that takes care of all of y'alls needs. The cell phones are satellite secure and they're encrypted. That means nobody will be listening to your conversations. But still, always be extra cautious." he warned.

Face and Reese nodded their heads to show that they understood.

"And also, gentlemen, never ever call us. When we need to speak to y'all, we'll call you. But, don't worry my new friends, in time that will change," Rico said, then continued. "We expect complete loyalty and trust from y'all. Any disloyalty or betrayal will result in the immediate death of both of y'all."

"And your loved ones," Jose added.

"Y'all don't have to ever worry about that," Face assured them. "There's a cop that worked for Hood..."

"We will no longer be doing business with any of Hood's organization. So, watch cha selves. Hood had a few friends that were very loyal to him. There will be a lot of hatred

towards y'all. So, always be extra careful," Rico said cutting Face off in mid-sentence.

"We know who they are and they'll be taken care of," Reese stated.

"Finally, how much can y'all handle right now?" Rico asked. Face looked over at Reese, then he turned back to Rico and said, "About thirty, I guess."

Everybody burst out with laughter, while Face and Reese stood there wondering what was so funny.

"He has a sense of humor, our new friend," Rico laughed, looking at his brother. "My friend we'll start you out at one hundred and fifty kilos. Then as you grow you can have more.

Call Roberto at the time it says on that paper and he'll have everything ready for you in the morning. Now, can y'all handle that?"

"Yeah, we can handle it," Face said.

Jose grabbed a pen and a piece of paper from the briefcase and wrote something down. "Here, this is the price we charge for each kilo," he said passing the slip of paper to Face.

Face looked at the price written on it and smiled. When he passed it to Reese, Reese did the same. With a bit of excitement in his voice, Face said, "We should be done in no time."

"That's what we expect," Rico replied.

After they all walked outside, Face and Reese both noticed the tinted black limousine parked right next to the Lexus. They watched as Jose and two of the body-guards walked

over and got inside, then Rico followed Face and Reese over to the Lexus.

"I want y'all to know that I have a lot of faith in you two. And I'm looking forward to doing big things together. My brother, Jose, still harbors some doubt and he's still a little

upset about what happened to Hood. But, something keeps telling me that y'all two will make both of us soon forget about Hood. The hunger in y'alls eyes don't lie," Rico said as he shook

both of their hands. "Now hurry and go back to Philadelphia, Sandy and Tasha have been worried sick about y'all," Rico said grinning.

Both Face and Reese stood there with dumbfounded expressions. They realized that the comment about their loved ones was the Gomez Brothers' way of letting them know that they had done extensive research and knew everything about them. They watched as Rico walked over to the waiting limousine and climbed inside. After the limousine had pulled off, they got inside the Lexus.

"We did it!" Reese said with excitement.

Face looked at his excited friend and calmly said, "Reese, this is only the beginning.

One hour later, the Denrich Apartment building...

When Face walked into his apartment Tasha jumped off the sofa and rushed towards him. They kissed while embracing in a long hug. Tears ran freely down Tasha's relieved face. For two stressful days she had been worried sick and going through it. Now, her king was back in her loving arms.

"I'm sorry. he said. "Never!" I'll never be away from you like that again," He picked her up in his powerful arms and carried her into the bedroom. After laying her across the bed, he took a step back and dropped to one knee. "Tasha, I want you to be my wife," he said.

Tasha sat up on the bed then walked over and kneeled down with Face. Her tears were relentless and her lips and hands both trembled. She stared into his face and said, "First, promise me one thing."

Face grabbed her trembling hands and said, "Just name it."

"Promise me that you will never cheat on me and never leave me like this again." she said through her tears.

"I promise you, Anything else?" Face asked.

Tasha smiled as she put her arms up around his neck and shoulders. "Yeah, I want you to give me days that I will always remember and nights that I will never forget."

Then once again they started passionately kissing.

* * *

Reese and Passion had just finished an intense round of fanatical love making. Their sweaty, exhausted bodies were laid out on top of the bed. Passion had her head laying on his chest. She was happy that Reese had finally came back home to her.

For two days she had been stressing and worrying and she had never felt more scared in her life.

"So Baby, you gotta be extra careful. That cop and his friend have been seen driving all around asking questions about me and you," Passion said in a concerned voice. "One of the girls at the club told me he was one of Hood's men. And so is the big guy he's been driving around with."

"Don't worry, me and Face will take care of everything. We know who the guy is," Reese said.

"What about the big guy he's been seen with?"

"We don't know him, but he is probably one of Hood's former bodyguards. He'll be taken care of, too," Reese assured her.

Reese rolled over and laid on top of Passion and softly kissed her on the lips. "Hood and his whole crew's reign is over with," he said with a smile on his face. Then he placed her legs on

top of his broad shoulders and smoothly entered her warm wet paradise. Moments later the sounds of lovemaking filled the bedroom.

CHAPTER 73

One month later...

In less than one month Face and Reese flipped the 150 Kilos five times. Since they had the best prices in the city, it was too hard for other drug dealers to compete. Plus, the product

was Grade-A cocaine at its finest. So now, many of the same people that bought their cocaine from Hood and Truck, were now buying it from Face and Reese. Money was constantly pouring in and every week Face was calling Roberto to exchange money for another shipment of cocaine. That made the Gomez brothers very happy.

Face and Reese were now major assets and Hood's memory was quickly dissipating.

Reese had gotten rid of the black Lexus and now he and Face were riding around in a brand new, silver, Range Rover. They had a few other automobiles that were used only for business only . They also made D.J. a part of the team and got him a new pager, cell phone, and a used Toyota Camry to get back and forth across town.

Tasha had moved most of her belongings from Momma's house and was now living with her fiancé full time. The wedding date was set and Face and Tasha were to be married in a little less than a year.

Their company, the T&F Real Estate firm, was doing very well; better than either of them had originally expected. Pamela had comfortably settled into her new job position and she was currently training her newest employee, Passion.

No longer an exotic dancer, Passion was excited about her new job. She promised herself that unless it was for Reese, she would never strip again. As for Jay, he was more miserable than he had ever been. At night, while Pamela peacefully slept, he would lay in bed crying and contemplating suicide. The reality that he'd never make love to Pamela again was slowly killing him. He yearned to be inside of her once more, but he knew that it would never happen. Deep down inside he felt his life was now meaningless, and the only way to make things better was to end it.

* * *

Reese and Tasha smiled from ear to ear as they happily sat down on opposite sides of Momma.

"Y'all better tell me what the hell is going on!" she said, looking back and forth between the two of them. Tasha went into her jacket pocket and took out a small photo of a beautiful white house. She passed the photo to Momma and said, "Momma, this is your new house."

"It's all paid for and you can move in a few days," Reese said.

Face, Pamela, Veronica, and D.J. were all standing around the living room with joy and happiness written all over their beaming faces. Momma sat back in total silence and for the first time in years her eyes welled up with tears, which slowly fell down her face. Everybody walked over and gave her hugs and kisses. For Momma, it was one of the happiest days of her entire life.

Since moving from Georgia, 35years ago, she had lived in the same old row house. The house was filled with lots of memories. Good, bad and ugly. But, Momma knew that it was now

time to move on and start a new life somewhere else. Somewhere much better and away from all the violence, poverty and drugs that had constantly surrounded her for all of her life.

Momma tearfully looked around at everyone's face and said, "I love all of y'all! Thank you so much!"

"We love you too, Momma," everyone said in unison. Then Momma reached over and grabbed her favorite device; the remote control.

"Alright, y'all can leave now. My soap's about to come on!" she said, as everyone burst out in laughter.

CHAPTER 74

April 9th, three days later...

Face and Reese had just returned to Philly from a trip to Miami. While there they met with Roberto, talked some business and also gave him a large sum of cash.

Inside one of their secret stash houses, Face, Reese and D.J. sat around a table counting a large pile of loose bills; hundreds, fifties, twenties, tens and fives. In front of each of them was a small money counting machine and plastic bags filled with thick rubber bands to tie up the money. A large, empty, green duffle bag was lying on the floor beside Face's chair. The secret stash house was one of three different houses they used to conduct business. They were all

owned by the T&F Real Estate company. Each house was in a different section of the city and they were all located in good quiet neighborhoods.

The men sat back counting money and enjoying the basketball game on a large screen color TV. The Philadelphia 76ers were getting blown out by Kobe Bryant and the Los Angeles Lakers. When the game finally ended,119 points win for L.A over the 97 points for the 76ers. The sports announcer came on the TV screen and said, "Well, the Sixers have lost their third straight game in a row. Maybe they'll rebound and pull out a victory tomorrow night against the New York Knicks. The Knicks superstar shooting-guard, Joey 'Slamdunk' Barnes is averaging twenty-eight points and thirteen rebounds per game. Hopefully, the Sixers will be able to slow Joey down and pull out a much needed victory."

Face and Reese looked at each other and smiled. No words needed to be said. Joey 'Slamdunk' Barnes was coming to town and they would make sure that he would never leave Philadelphia alive.

Southwest Philly...

Pamela was at work and two nurses had just left Jay alone in the house. When the doorbell rang, Jay rolled his wheelchair over to the front door, "Who is it?" he yelled out.

"It's me Jay, Kyle," a voice said from the other side of the door.

Jay quickly opened the door and allowed the man to come inside. He closed the door and they shook hands. Kyle was Jay's younger friend; the same man that had gotten out of Jay's truck just seconds before Killa-D and Snake shot it up. Kyle was no longer working for Jay, but they still remained close friends.

Now, Kyle was working for Face and Reese and was selling cocaine out of the same house where he used to sell weed for Jay. Kyle lifted up his tee-shirt and took out a .357 Bulldog…a snubbed nosed revolver and passed it to Jay and said, "Here you go, Jay. But, why do you need that?"

"I have to take care of some very important business," Jay replied, as he laid the pistol in his lap.

"I made sure it was loaded, just like you asked," Kyle smiled.

"Thanks Kyle. Is everything going well with you?" Jay asked changing the subject.

"Yeah. Thanks for hooking me up with Face. I'm making a killin'," he said, appreciatively.

"No problem. Face will take good care of you. He's a good dude," Jay told him.

When Kyle opened the front door and walked outside, Jay watched as he walked over to a new white Jaguar and climbed inside. After Kyle had pulled off , Jay closed the door. He picked up the gun and just stared at it. He had already written his suicide note. Now, the only thing left to do was to summon up enough courage to actually pull the trigger.

Later that night...

The black Yukon Denali drove down the street and slowed down as it passed Momma's house. Ron Perry, Big C and an unidentified man were all inside the truck. A few blocks away Ron Perry pulled his truck over and parked.

"Tomorrow night, it's going down," he said, looking at both of them.

"We'll be ready," Big C said, as he and the other man got out of the truck and closed the door.

Ron Perry watched as the two men climbed into a gray Ford Explorer. Moments later they made a U-turn and drove off in the opposite direction. With a sly grin, Ron Perry pulled away from the curb and headed for his office at the 18th District's Police Station.

As the Ford Explorer drove up Walnut Street, Big C and his friend were inside talking. "Why you hate that nigga, Reese so much?" The guy asked, as they stopped at a red light.

"Because of something he did to me a long time ago," Big C replied.

"What he do?"

"I don't wanna talk about it. Just know that it's personal between me and this nigga Reese," Big C said in an angry tone.

The man looked over at Big C and just shook his head. When the light turned green he pulled off, thinking to himself that the worst place a person could be was on Big C's bad side.

* * *

Reese laid back in bed with one of his arms wrapped around Passion and the other wrapped around her girlfriend, White Chocolate. They were all naked and had just finished a wild round of sex. White Chocolate never turned down an opportunity to join Passion and Reese in a threesome. Not only were they good friends but the sex was always amazing, and Passion didn't mind sharing Reese with another woman. Not even a beautiful white woman like White Chocolate. She was confident in herself and secure with their relationship. Plus, whatever Reese asked her to do, she never hesitated to get it done.

"So, are y'all two ready for tomorrow?" Reese asked.

"Yeah, Daddy, we got this," White Chocolate said, as she ran a long manicured fingernail idly around his chest.

"Ita be a piece of cake," she added with a smile.

Passion rolled over and laid on top of Reese's hard muscular body and kissed him softly on the lips. "Don't worry baby, if he like pussy, he's as good as got. And I don't know no man who can resist both flavors at once. Chocolate and Vanilla, please," Passion said teasingly.

The Denrich Apartments...

Face looked over at Tasha and watched as she peacefully slept, then he turned his head and continued to stare at the ceiling. His intuitive mind was filled with many thoughts. He thought about how he had come so far in the game in such a short period of time. Pictures of Hood, Mouse, Truck and a few others flashed in and out of his head. Face knew that each one of them had strived for the three things that every hustler craved; Money, Power and Success. But they had all fallen short and became victims of the game that they craved and loved.

"I'm gonna make it," Face whispered to himself. "I'm gonna be the man who wins!"

With a big smile on his face he turned and wrapped his arms around Tasha's body and happily closed his eyes.

CHAPTER 75

The next day, Laredo, Texas...

Laredo, Texas is a relatively small town in southwest Texas and is less than an hour from the Mexican border. On a privately owned ranch, not far from the Rio Grande River, Roberto Chevez stood watching as a large white food truck backed carefully into the huge barn.

The three workers got out of the truck and rushed straight to the back of the barn. One of Roberto's workers quickly closed the barn door then ran behind the truck with the other three workers. The back doors of the truck's trailer were quickly unlocked and opened. Then all four men climbed inside.

After moving all the brown boxes of canned goods aside, the four workers saw hundreds of large black food boxes stacked up in the back of the truck. But, this cargo wasn't just food. It also contained a large cocaine shipment straight from Mexico; so far, it was the third one of the day.

Roberto's good friends worked at the U.S. and Mexican border control and was paid top dollar to make sure it entered into the U.S. territory unscathed. As the workers unloaded the black boxes filled with kilos of Columbian cocaine Roberto dialed a number on his cell phone. On the second ring a voice answered.

"Hello? Roberto, is everything okay?" Rico asked. "Yes Boss, the last shipment of the day just came through. I'm headed to Miami next, to make sure everything goes well there."

"Good, I will see you in a few days. How's our young friends doing in Philly?"

"Very good. Just as good as the last one," Roberto said.

"Okay, my friend, continue to keep me posted. I'll let my brother know that everything is going well. Goodbye," Rico said, then hung up the phone.

After the workers had removed all the boxes of cocaine, the doors on the truck were closed and locked. Then, one of the workers opened the barn doors and stood back watching as

the truck drove out.

A half an hour later Roberto was seated in the back of a tinted Mercedes Benz and was being driven to the airport by one of his workers. His next destination was Miami. Being the top underboss in a powerful drug organization was a 24 hour a day job. And Roberto enjoyed every single moment of it.

Inside the offices of the T&F Real Estate firm...

Pamela sat at her desk and looked on as Tasha argued with someone on the phone. "Listen here Mr. Reynolds, I've checked all the records. You are seventy-five thousand dollars behind on your taxes and the property is about to be foreclosed on by the bank. I'm willing to take this mess off your hands and still let you walk away with a small profit. Now, either you're going to agree to my terms, or I'll take my offer off the table and find another property somewhere else. Now, what's it going to be?" Tasha demanded.

After a long pause Mr. Reynolds said, "Alright, you win. I'm on my way down there now, just have all the paperwork ready for me to sign."

"Don't you worry. Everything will be ready when you get here and so will your check," Tasha promised, then she hung up the phone.

Pamela stood up from her seat and excitedly rushed over and gave Tasha a hug. "You did it girl! You did it!" she said happily.

Tasha had just convinced Mr. Reynolds to sell his run-down apartment building in North Philadelphia. The dilapidated three story building was located a few blocks away from Temple University. What Mr. Reynolds didn't know was that Tasha had already had a private meeting with school officials and Temple University was currently interested in buying old buildings to renovate for student housing. Once the deal with Mr. Reynolds was finalized, Tasha's next move was to sell the property to Temple University and walk away with a healthy profit.

Later that night...

Face and Reese patiently waited inside the tan colored Dodge Caravan. Two hours earlier they had both sat in expensive front row seats inside the First Union Center watching as the 76ers finally snapped their three game losing streak with a win against the New York Knicks.

In a losing effort Joey 'Slamdunk' Barnes had an unbelievable game; 33 points, 19 rebounds, 4 blocks, and 9 assists. But neither Face or Reese were impressed.

The tinted Caravan was parked directly across the street from the Egypt Night Club. Face and Reese had been setting in the van for the past hour with their pistols loaded and tucked under their belts and hidden beneath their tee-shirts. They watched the boisterous crowd of party goers as they entered into the popular club.

Inside the club's crowded VIP section, athletes, entertainers, and hoards of beautiful women floated around meeting and greeting one another. The club was packed to capacity and the music was loud and intoxicating. Joey Barnes had just purchased a $200 bottle of Louis Roederer's Cristal Champagne. When he walked back over to his small private table a beautiful black woman was sitting there smiling and waiting for him. Joey sat down beside her and placed his arm around her shoulder.

"So, Passion, what was you saying before I left?" he said showing his pearly whites.

"I was saying that you're my favorite basketball player in the whole world," Passion said, as she rubbed her hand up and down his thigh.

"So, you like me better than Jordan?" Joey asked.

"Way better," she lied convincingly. "Me and my girlfriend love you," Passion said.

"Is that right?" Joey said, leaning over and kissing Passion's neck.

"Yeah, and we share everything."

Joey stopped kissing and looked into Passion's eyes, "Why don't you call her, then? And we can all go back to my hotel room?"

"I don't have to call her. She's right over there," she said pointing to the tall, attractive white woman sitting at the bar. White Chocolate was seated at the bar with three black male admirers fighting for her attention.

Joey had spotted her earlier and wanted to say something to her, but after seeing the breathtaking body on Passion, he had approached her instead. Still, like most black men he had

a curious desire for white women.

"That's your girl friend?" he asked in surprise.

"Yeah, her name is Tiffney. She's my best friend and college roommate," Passion said with a grin. "And, like I said, we share everything," she added.

Joey's lustful eyes watched as Passion got up from her seat and walked over to the bar. The jeans Passion wore accentuated her perfectly round ass and the thought of stripping off all her clothes and fucking the shit out of her made him hard with anticipation. He had slept with many groupies before but none of them had a body like Passion's. And the thought of having Passion along with her attractive white girlfriend would be even better; two more names to add to his long list of sex partners.

After Passion whispered something in White Chocolate's ear, she got up from her bar stool and together they smiled as they walked over and joined Joey at his table.

"Joey, this is my friend, Tiffney and she's a bigger fan of yours than I am," Passion said introducing them.

"Glad to meet you Tiffney," he said staring into her piercing blue eyes. "So, now that everyone has met, let's take this bottle of champagne and get up out of here," Joey said excitedly.

"My hotel is not far from here."

"Sounds fine with me," White Chocolate said as they all stood up and headed toward the VIP's exit.

* * *

Jay rolled his wheelchair around to the opposite side of the bed and watched as Pamela peacefully slept. For a few silent moments he sat there staring at her beautiful face, lost in the memory of all the sex they used to share. As his eyes filled with tears he turned his wheelchair around and rolled out of the bedroom.

When Jay entered the bathroom he closed the door and reached underneath his tee shirt and pulled out the loaded .357 Bulldog revolver. He had already left the suicide letter on top of his pillow. In total silence he sat thinking about his miserable life and his tears continued to fall down his wide open eyes. He placed the stubby barrel of the pistol into the deepness of his mouth.

Pamela opened her eyes and turned over in bed. When she saw that Jay wasn't sleeping beside her she quickly sat up. She noticed the small white sheet of paper lying on top of his pillow.

She grabbed the note and immediately started reading, 'Pamela, I want you to know that I love you more than any words I could ever say. You are a true queen, Pamela. A one of a kind woman. I know you'll be very mad at me for doing this, but I honestly can't go on living like this. I'm sorry, but death is the only way for me to escape my miserable life - Jay.'

"Jay!" Pamela yelled as she leaped from the bed.

BOOOOOMM!

The loud blast stopped Pamela dead in her tracks. She froze completely. As the tears began falling down her terrified face, her hands and legs started to tremble uncontrollably. Fear and confusion swept throughout her body and after a long sigh she walked toward the bathroom. Her heart was pounded rapidly and her chest felt like it could explode.

When she approached the bathroom door she grabbed the knob and slowly turned it. She pushed the door open and stood there in the doorway. What Pamela saw was like a scene in a horror movie. The back of Jay's head was completely blown off! Pieces of brain fragments, flesh and his skull were splattered all over the walls.

Pamela stood there wide eyed as she looked at Jay's collapsed corpse. The .357 was lying on the floor in front of the wheel chair. Finally, she slowly turned away and walked back to the bedroom and sat on the bed staring straight ahead of her – looking at nothing in particular. She couldn't believe that Jay went out that way. Pamela was angry, filled with pain and grief and she was totally confused. After wiping her tears away she reached for the phone and dialed 911.

* * *

The Ford Explorer pulled up at the corner of 29th and Dauphin Street. Big C was behind the wheel and Ron Perry was sitting in the passenger seat. Both of them had black ski-masks laying in their laps and loaded glock 17.9mm automatics were under their tee-shirts. The back door of the truck opened up and a man got inside. He closed the door and sat back, as Big C pulled away from the curb.

"You ready, Zeno?" Ron Perry asked.

"I'm always ready for murder," he laughed.

Zeno was another one of Hood's former street soldiers. He was a ruthless killer from North Philly, and a loyal friend to his former boss. As the truck headed back towards West Philly, Zeno sat back loading bullets into his .40 caliber pistol. He lived for murder and mayhem, and the thought of killing two people tonight made his trigger finger itch with anticipation.

CHAPTER 76

Outside Club Egypt...

The all black Bentley Azure pulled up and Passion and White Chocolate both smiled when they climbed inside. Most of the party goers were inside the club, so Joey didn't have to worry about signing any more autographs. Passion sat up front while White Chocolate got in the back seat. When Joey made the quick u-turn and drove down Delaware Avenue there was a smile as big as day plastered all over his face because tonight he was looking forward to a wild and lustful threesome. He simply couldn't wait to get both these women in his hotel room.

As he headed towards the Marriot Hotel, Passion quietly sat back holding onto her purse. Then she grabbed her stomach and said, "I feel like I'm going to throw-up! Pull over!" she added, seriously.

"Hold up! Don't throw up in my ride!" Joey said, as he quickly pulled over onto the side of the road.

"Girl, I told you not to drink so much!" White Chocolate said. "You know how you get!"

Passion opened the door and stepped out of the car. Joey opened his door and got out as well. When he ran around the other side of the car, Passion was bent over holding her

stomach. "You all right?" Joey asked concerned. "I don't remember you drinking all that much," he added.

White Chocolate opened the back door of the car and stepped out of the car. Inside her hand was a loaded .380 pistol and she slowly approached Joey from behind. At the same time a tinted Dodge Caravan pulled up behind Joey's Bentley. When Joey turned around to see who it was, White Chocolate had the .380 pistol pointed directly at his head.

"What the fuck is goin on?" he asked.

"Shut the fuck up you raping muthafucker!" Passion said as she pulled a .22 caliber pistol from her purse and stood straight up.

"Y'all two bitches set me up!" Joey angrily said, standing there with both his hands in the air, watching as the two men got out of the Caravan.

"Get the fuck in the van!" Reese told him.

"Look man, just tell me how much money y'all want..."

"Nigga, shut the fuck up and get in the van!" Face said cutting him off in mid sentence.

"Bitches!" Joey mumbled under his breath as he walked over to the van.

With his .9mm to Joey's back Reese pushed Joey inside the van, then got in beside him and closed the sliding door.

Passion and White Chocolate got into Joey's car and drove down the dark street. Then Face walked over and got back inside the van. When he got back inside Joey was handcuffed and sitting on the back seat with Reese.

"Look, just let me know how much y'all want!" he pleaded as Face drove in the darkness of the night.

Joey looked at both men and even though neither one of them spoke a single word, he knew that they were serious and feared for his life. His intuition told him this wasn't a typical robbery/kidnapping in exchange for money. As sweat from nerves and fear poured from his body his breathe began to run a race with his heart.

Twenty minutes later the van parked in a dark secluded area, underneath the Benjamin Franklin Bridge. A few feet away was Joey's Bentley Azure. The doors on the van opened and Joey was pushed to the ground. Face and Reese stood over his tall, slim body with their pistols aimed at his head.

"Please man, don't kill me! I'll give y'all whatever y'all want!" he begged, cried and pleaded.

"We don't want shit from you, you coward!" Reese said in an angry tone.

"Joey, do you remember a girl named Tasha?" Face asked.

"Who? Man I know lots of girls named Tasha! Just tell me what's this all about!" he cried out.

"It's about the Tasha that you raped! Her name is Tasha Daniels, muthafucker! Do you remember now? You raped her inside your truck, you bastard!" Face shouted.

The old memory instantly came back to Joey. He sat on the ground shaking his head in confusion and fear. "She gave it to me!" he lied in desperation.

"Stop lying muthafucker! You took it!" Reese fumed. "And now we gonna take something from you," he added.

"Your life!" Face said, as both he and Reese aimed their guns at Joey's head and squeezed the triggers. Tht! Tht! Tht! Tht! Tht! Tht! Six quick near silent bullets entered and exited

Joey's head and chest. Face and Reese watched as his body laid on the cold ground. In the darkness of the night they got back inside the van and drove off, leaving behind another

dead victim who got what he deserved.

West Philly...

D.J. was inside the living room laying across the sofa watching TV. Momma's and his personal belongings were all stacked up against the wall in large brown boxes. They were planning to move into their new home in Springfield, Pennsylvania, early the next morning.

Just like Momma, D.J. was also looking forward to getting out of the city and enjoying a change of scenery. As his eyes started to tire and close he heard the sound of voices. He sat up on the sofa and looked toward the front door. As soon as he stood up, three armed and masked men crashed in the front door and quickly ran inside.

D.J. was completely caught off guard. It happened so fast that he didn't know if he should run or scream. But before he could make any decisions, all three men had already aimed their pistols at him and began firing bullets into his unprotected body. He was dead before his lifeless body slumped hard to the floor.

"Upstairs!" one of the men yelled.

Hearing the loud commotion coming from downstairs, Momma quickly woke from her slumber, sat up in bed, and reached for and grabbed her shotgun-Betsy. Momma had ole' Betsy cocked and aimed, ready to shoot the first person that came through the door. Suddenly her bedroom door was kicked open and a tall, masked man, dressed in all black was standing there holding a pistol.

BOOOOOMMM!

Momma pulled the trigger and shot the man square in the chest. In an instant, the powerful impact completely knocked him off his feet. But, before Momma could get herself and Betsy ready for the next intruder, the other two masked men rushed into the bedroom firing their pistols.

Momma was shot twice in the stomach. Her old body fell to the floor with Betsy dropping beside her.

"Oh God! Oh God!" Momma cried out feeling the hot burning sensation now running throughout her elderly body.

In the fetal position Momma laid on the floor holding her bleeding stomach. She could feel her 67 earthly years quickly coming to a tragic end.

"Oh God! Oh God, please help me!" she painfully said.

Ron Perry stood over Momma's dying body and grabbed a handful of her hair. Lifting her body high off the ground by her hair, he pointed his glock at her head and said, "I'm sorry, but God ain't here to help you right now!" He shot her in the side of the head then he let Momma's dead body slump to the bedroom floor.

"Come on Big C, let's get the fuck outta here!" Ron Perry said, and both of them turned and ran out of the bedroom, passed their dead friend Zeno, straight down the stairs and out the front door to the waiting Ford Explorer pickup truck.

CHAPTER 77

One month later...

The tragic deaths of Momma, D.J. and Jay left everyone in a dark and gloomy mood. However, no one seemed more hurt than Reese. For weeks he had distanced himself from everyone, trying to come to terms with his loss. His sadness was profound! He saw his grandmother and D.J. as his only remaining true family.

At Momma and D.J.'s funeral, Face had to grab and comfort him from his loud, screaming outbursts. His eyes were bloodshot and glassy from the lack of sleep and his heart carried an indescribable feeling of loss and pain.

Reese knew he would never rest until he found and killed the people responsible for murdering Momma and D.J. He and Face already suspected it was members of Hood's former drug organization but, they had no solid proof…Yet. And finding Zeno's dead body inside the house proved that Zeno wasn't working on his own. He could have been hired by someone else and was killed by Momma in the process. Either way Reese and Face swore to find and kill whoever was responsible.

They also felt that Detective Ron Perry and his friend Big C were somehow involved in the killings. Now, Face was using all his power and influence to get them back for what they had done. It was personal. Very personal! Ron Perry and Big C were now wanted men and neither Face or Reese would rest until they were both dead.

The Range Rover drove slowly through the cemetery, headed towards Momma's and D.J.'s grave sites. Inside the Holy Cross Cemetery their caskets had been buried right beside one another. When the Range Rover stopped, Face and Reese both got out and walked over to the large headstones and stared in silence and disbelief. Reese fell to his knees and put his face in his hands and started to cry. A river of tears streamed silently through his fingers and ran in rivulets down his arms and dripped from his elbows. He slowly looked up at Face and said, "It's time for my enemies to feel all my pain, Face. Ain't no mercy for none of them!"

Face fell to his knees beside Reese and put his arm around his shoulders.

"I'ma kill'em!" Reese shouted out.

Face looked deep into Reese's watery, tired eyes and said, "Reese everything will be all right. Ron Perry and this guy, Big C are both on our shit list and death is the only way off of it! Just remember, the way we think will determine the way we walk. And the way we walk will determine the way we succeed. And we will succeed, I promise."

After they both stood up from the ground, Face watched as Reese stepped forward and gently kiss both tombstones.

"I love you, Momma," Reese said before he turned and walked back over to his Range Rover. When he and Face got back inside the truck, Reese slowly pulled off and drove down the small dusty cemetery road.

On the back seat of Reese's truck there was a large black suitcase with a million and a half dollars in cash inside. They were headed to Atlanta, Georgia where their good friend Roberto Chevez was patiently waiting at one of the Gomez's many safe houses. The Gomez Brothers had safe houses all around the country; Miami, Florida, Laredo, Texas, Atlanta, Georgia, New York City, Los Angeles, California, Detroit, Michigan, Baltimore, Maryland, and other places that were too numerous to mention.

As Reese drove out of the cemetery he looked at Face and said, "Thanks Face. Thanks for everything."

Face placed his hand on Reese's shoulder and smiled. "What are brothers for?" he answered sincerely, then watched as Reese returned the smile and pressed the play button on the CD player. Seconds later the powerful voice of The Notorious B.I.G flowed out of the speakers.

Inside the FBI Building at 6th and Arch Street...

Agent Powaski stood in front of the white board looking at a pyramid of faces. Since Hood's murder there had been a major shake-up in the streets of Philadelphia. New faces and names emerged from nowhere. But among the flock of new young drug dealers, two new names circulated heavily on the streets; Norman 'Face' Smith and Maurice Daniels.

Agent Powaski walked over to a chair and sat down beside his partner. "So, what cha think McDonald?" he said.

Agent McDonald shrugged his shoulders and said, "Right now there's only a lot of talk and guessing. We still have to wait for awhile to find out the whole truth about this guy Face and his partner, Reese."

"But, our sources on the streets are saying that Face is the man," Powaski argued.

"Maybe so, but we still need more proof," McDonald replied, as he sipped his cup of hot coffee.

"Where the hell did this kid come from?" Powaski said.

"No one knows and he has absolutely no juvenile or adult criminal record. He is squeaky clean," McDonald replied.

"How about his partner?"

"He's had a few run ins with the law but, nothing real serious. His grandmother and younger brother were recently murdered inside their West Philly home about a month ago. And one of Hood's former street soldiers was found dead inside the house as well."

"There's something big going on that we know nothing about. And I don't like it!"

"Don't worry, partner. In time we'll both find out everything we need to know. But right now, we just have to wait and see," Agent McDonald said.

Agent Powaski stood up, walked over to the white board, and snatched down the picture of Face. Then he held it in his hand and just stared at it.

Northwest Philadelphia...

The elderly white man opened his front door and let Ron Perry in. He'll be right down," the man said smiling.

Ron Perry watched as the old man turned and walked away. Moments later Lil' Robbie was smiling as he walked down the stairs. They met at the foot of the stairs and gave each other a long warm hug. Since Hood's tragic death, Ron Perry would occasionally drive to Britney's parent's home and check on Lil' Robbie and Arianna.

"Where's your sister?"

"She's out food shopping with Grandma," Robbie replied, as they walked over to the couch and sat down.

Nine year old Robbie was tall for his age and was the spitting image of his father, Hood. "Did you find out who killed my parents?" Robbie asked curiously.

After a long sigh, Ron Perry said, "If I tell you Robbie, you must keep it between me and you."

"Alright," Robbie promised, anxiously waiting. "I believe the person who murdered your parents was your older brother. His name is Face," Ron Perry said, watching as Robbie's eyes filled with tears.

"Is that's my real mother's other son," he tearfully asked.

"Yeah, Robbie, the son she didn't abandon. The one she loved," Ron Perry replied.

"When...When...I...I was little, I remember him. He used to hold me a lot," Robbie cried.

Ron Perry reached out and gave Robbie a hug. "I just wanted you to know the truth, Robbie."

After they talked for a short while, Robbie watched Ron Perry walk out the front door and get inside his truck. Then, he ran back upstairs into his bedroom and closed the door to finish crying.

Inside his truck Ron Perry looked at Big C and smiled. "I told the kid," he said, pulling away from the curb.

"Good, now Face will one day add a new enemy to his list. His own brother," Big C said as he and Ron Perry burst with laughter.

CHAPTER 78

June 16, 2000, Honolulu, Hawaii, one year later...

Inside a lavish and beautifully decorated beach house situated on two acres of land, Face and the love of his life, Tasha, were married. The two million dollar home was owned by the Gomez brothers; one of the many they had situated around the world. They had allowed Face and Tasha to use it for this special occasion and only their immediate family members were invited to the private wedding ceremony.

The Gomez brothers also allowed Face, his new wife, and their close family members the luxury of using their personal yacht. Face was now considered 'family' and there was nothing within their power that the Gomez brothers would not do for him.

He and Reese were bringing in millions of dollars a month, helping the Gomez brothers expand their already powerful drug cartel. But what had impressed the Gomez brothers more than anything else was Face's loyalty and ambition to succeed. They saw such determination in Face...determination that they had never seen in anyone so young.

At just 20 years old, Face was in a league of his very own. Not only was he a tall and handsome young man, he was also humble and caring. And when it came to handling his business he was always meticulous and cautious. He only trusted a few people, and he kept his circle small and tight. Face learned from many men that came before him. He studied their strengths and their weaknesses. This was one of the reasons why he never put his name on anything and his phone conversations were always brief and coded. He also stayed abreast of the world around him.

Face enjoyed watching CNN and read several newspapers a day. He liked the Wall Street Journal,

Washington Post, and the New York Times. He was like a sponge who soaked up every vital piece of information that would strengthen his intuitive young mind. Although he liked sports and entertainment, his focus was primarily on politics and even philosophy. He read about men like Rupert Murdoch, Steve Forbes, Steven Jobbs and Bill Gates; all powerful billionaires. He also read and studied the lives of famous drug kingpins like Pablo Escobar, the king of cocaine; Freeway Ricky Ross, the king of crack; and Aaron Jones, the leader of Philly's own J.B.M. (Junior Black Mafia). Face read about these men and so many others and he was destined to one day out do them all.

After their wedding and three week honeymoon, Face and Tasha flew back to Philly on the Gomez's private jet. Reese was waiting at the airport inside a tinted black limousine. When Face and Tasha had got inside the limo Reese gave them both a long hug. While Face was away on his honeymoon, Reese had been running things in his absence. Face noticed the big smile on Reese's face and said, "What is it?"

As Tasha laid her head in Face's lap, Reese leaned over and cupped his hand around Face's ear, "We got Big C! And you won't believe who he is!" Reese whispered. Face looked at Reese's beaming expression and nodded his head. He smiled and relaxed in the plush soft leather seat and ran his fingers through his wife's long black hair.

Bala Cynwyd, Pa...

Forty five minutes later the limousine pulled up and double parked in front of a beautiful new home. The house was owned by the T&F Real Estate firm. Face had Tasha purchased a few luxury cars and homes in the company's name. They had homes in Drexel Hill,

Springfield, and in Cheltenham, Pa., and they also owned an elegant condo in Center City Philadelphia.

Not only was Face's illegal drug business prospering, but the T&F real estate firm was doing extremely well. In just a short time, Tasha had turned their small real estate company into one of the most successful companies in Philadelphia. At twenty-four years old she was highly respected by her peers and had already established a reputation as a shrewd and clever business woman. Her colleagues loved her, while her competitors showed envy and fear. And just like her husband, she would allow nothing to stand in her path to success.

After everyone had gotten out of the limousine, Face gave Tasha a passionate kiss and hug and watched as she walked into her new home. The limo driver followed her inside the house, carrying two large suitcases.

When the limo driver returned, he got back into the limo and drove away. Face and Reese walked over to a brand new all white Lincoln Navigator and got inside. Reese got behind the wheel while Face rode shotgun. Reese started the engine and headed for a house in the North-Philly section of the city, near Broad and Susquehanna Avenue.

* * *

Inside the master bedroom, Tasha walked over to a large window and looked outside. The morning sky was a crisp blue with a few sluggish clouds passing overhead. The master bedroom overlooked the tennis court and surrounding woods. The lavishly built home had six bedrooms, an exercise room, and an elaborate entertainment room, complete with a theatre, bar and video games.

Tasha stood there letting the warm wind blow against her face. At that moment she had never known such happiness. She rubbed her hands around her plump round belly and smiled. She was three months pregnant with Face's first child. Their baby was due in mid December and neither of them could wait for its arrival.

She turned from the window and walked toward the room sized walk in closet. Names like Jimmy Choos, Manolo Blahniks, Versace, Dolce & Gabbana and Louis Vuitton graced the closet's racks and shelves. They were living a life that many had only dreamt of, and deep down in their hearts, Face and Tasha knew that this was only the beginning.

North Philly ....

Inside the basement of a small row house, Big C was tied to a long wooden table. He could feel the walls inside the room closing in on him. Two days earlier he had been seen by two of Face's top street lieutenants as he came out of the crime controlled Richard Allen Projects.

Being taken by gunpoint, they brought Big C to the house and held him there until Reese showed up. Reese was enjoying another wonderful threesome with Passion and White Chocolate when he was told the good news about Big C's capture. He quickly jumped out of bed, got dressed and rushed over to the house.

When Reese finally saw who Big C was, he could hardly believe his own eyes. It had been well over ten years since the last time they laid eyes on each other. But neither one of them

had forgotten their last meeting; that day at the playground when he, Face and D.J. had beat Big C down to a pulp. Back then though, he had been known by one name, Chub; the neighborhood

bully.

Face followed Reese down the basement stairs and over to the large man who was tied down and lying on a table. "Chub!" Face asked, in disbelief. "Chub is Big C?" he said as he repeated his question in a confused voice.

Reese eagerly nodded his head and said, "Yup!"

Face stood there in a state of awe. "Did he say anything about Ron Perry?" he asked.

"Not a word. He still think he's a tough guy," Reese grinned.

Face reached down and snatched the silver duct tape from over his mouth. "Either you tell us everything you know about Ron Perry, or you die!" Face told him.

Big C looked up at the two men with a devilish smirk. "Fuck both y'all cowards! Y'all gonna kill me anyway!' he added.

Face turned and looked at his two armed men, "Y'all two can leave now. Me and Reese got this," he said.

They watched as the two men left the basement. Then Face looked over at Reese and said, "Where are the knives?"

Reese smiled and walked over to a chair and picked up two sharp jungle machetes and a white pillow case. He walked back over to Face and handed him one of the machetes.

"What the fuck are..." Face slapped the duct tape back over Chub's mouth, cutting off anything else he had to say. Then, he watched as Reese placed the pillowcase over Chub's head. They stood there momentarily looking down at their long lost enemy.

"You ready, Reese?"

"I been ready!" Reese replied as he raised his arm with the machete clutched tightly in his hand.

Later that night...

A dark colored Buick Regal drove up and stopped in front of the 18th District's Police Station at 55th and

Pine Street. A short brown skinned man quickly got out of the car. In his hands he carried a closed brown box with the words 'For Detective Ron Perry' written on top of the box with a black magic marker. The man sat the box down on the front step and rushed back to his car and quickly sped off down the dark street.

An hour later police officers and members of the bomb squad unit had the area secured. They stood around watching the remote controlled robot identify the contents of the mysterious box. After the robot completed its x-ray examination of the box, it was determined by the bomb technicians that the contents were not explosives.

The next thing they did was check for biological and radiological contaminants. Those tests also came back negative. Therefore, the decision was made by the lieutenant on call to destroy the box. Destroying it entailed inserting a spherical explosive chamber that would annihilate the box using a highly explosive device. The sphere was put into place and within minutes the robot was maneuvered into position. All systems were go and they were ready to lift the box onto the robot's coffin.

As the robot slowly and steadily picked up the box, the bottom of the box fell open and a human head fell to the ground. The group of police officers all stood there in total disbelief and stared in awe at the severed head. Ron Perry turned and walked away, and inside he was fuming with rage. Another friend was dead and there was nothing he could do about it.

As he walked toward his office, Ron Perry made a promise to himself that he wouldn't rest until Face and Reese were both dead and their entire organization was destroyed.

CHAPTER 79

Early May, six years later...

The past six years had gone by in a flash. Now, Face and Reese were the two young bosses of one of the most powerful organized drug syndicates in the country. With the Gomez brothers supplying them with unlimited amounts of drugs and protection, they were nearly unstoppable. Every month they were receiving large shipments of cocaine, between 500 and 6,000 kilos, and between 100 and 300 kilos of pure, uncut, China White heroin. Face had become so big that he now supplied drugs to six other U.S. states; Camden and Trenton, New Jersey, Baltimore, Maryland, Youngstown, Ohio, Pittsburgh, Pennsylvania and Detroit, Michigan. The good thing about this was...Face kept his circle so small and tight that only those that needed to know, knew he was the mastermind behind it all.

Face had top notch attorneys overseeing his legal businesses and accountants oversaw his finances. With offshore accounts in the Cayman Islands and Belize, there were only a handful

of people who knew his true wealth.

Face was now the number one asset for the Gomez brothers. Not only did they supply him with drugs, but they also supplied his organization with weapons, advanced security equipment, police scanners, night vision equipment and sophisticated surveillance and gear.

The T&F Real Estate Firm was now operating out of a twenty story building in downtown Philadelphia. The company occupied the top two floors and Tasha managed the day to day operations. T&F Real Estate was now one of the largest black owned corporations on the East Coast. With over a hundred million dollars in assets under her management, T&F Real Estate owned and operated more than 3000 properties in four states. Tasha was the Chief Executive Officer and business strategist, overseeing such functions as retail branch development, mergers and acquisitions, and development and relationship management. Pamela was now the Vice President of the company helping Tasha with the day-to-day operations that kept T&F Real Estate on top.

East Hampton, Long Island, New York...

The large French Normandy home sat on an acre of property just off prestigious Hither Lane. The five million dollar home had a master suite, four guest suites, a magnificent living room, a den, a formal dining room and a media room. It also had two large kitchens with the second kitchen being located right beside the heated slate pool, inside it's extravagant pool house.

The luxurious home was another property owned by the T&F Real Estate Firm. It was a place where Face often came to gather his thoughts. He had small hidden video cameras installed that constantly monitored the house and its surrounding property. Each camera had a motion detector that would send an e-mail and override whatever Face was doing on the computer. It also had a recording of Tasha's voice that would announce if an intruder was on the property and gave the exact location where the intruder could be located. The cameras, once tripped, would also begin recording the actions of the trespasser and could record hours of video on the computer system's hard drive. They also included a constant 'real-time' time and date readout.

Face sat back on the sofa with his eyes glued to CNN. He had just learned that the President had appointed C.W. Watson as the new head of the Anti-Drug Commission. His new job was to coordinate with the heads of the FBI, DEA, ATF and the Department of Homeland Security to ferret out and destroy or arrest any and all drug traffickers in the United States. Then to back track their sources and assist foreign law enforcement in destroying them wherever they were found.

Face watched the entire program with great interest. When it had ended he turned off the TV and took out his cell phone. He dialed a number and someone answered on the first ring.

"Hello my good friend, what can I do for you?" Rico said.

"Did you just watch CNN?"

"Yes, me and my brother both did. Don't worry. It is nothing," Rico assured him.

"I think the new guy in charge might be serious about changing things. Maybe just to impress his boss," Face stated.

"It is all political, my friend; just an illusion to manipulate the public once again. This new guy is just another government pawn. One with a hard bark and a soft bite!" Rico said with

a knowing laugh.

"He mentioned a list of names that he had..." Face started.

"Don't worry yourself, my friend," Rico interrupted. "We will continue to stay five steps ahead of them. 9-11 didn't stop us. In fact after September 11th things have gotten much better for us. Do you know why?"

"No, tell me," Face said.

"Because, it's all a game my friend. A game between the rich and poor. They allow certain things to happen so that it will benefit them. Because of us their judges, lawyers,

probation officers and federal agents will all have jobs. Don't forget the horribly overcrowded U.S. Prison systems that are filled with millions of our fellow citizens. I told you before, my friend, it is all big business.

Bigger than you and I could ever imagine," Rico answered seriously.

"So, you don't think this new guy, C.W. Watson is a real threat?" Face asked seriously.

"Not at all," Rico replied. "I will see you tomorrow and we will talk some more about this, okay? Take care," Rico said then disconnected the call.

Face closed his cell phone and stood up from the sofa. He walked over to the door and went outside. Parked in front of the mansion was a silver Mercedes Benz SLR McLaren Supercharged Coupe. Face walked over and climbed inside the car. Moments later he was cruising down the long winding driveway towards the street. He was headed back to Philadelphia to be with his wife and two young children.

* * *

Detective Ron Perry walked into the Federal Building lobby and got into one of the elevators. He pressed the button for the fifth floor and watched as the doors slowly closed. A bit of nervous tension lingered in his body. An hour earlier he received a message to come to the Federal Building and meet with two FBI agents. He had no idea why the Feds wanted to see him.

As the elevator climbed up the shaft, his mind raced with guilty thoughts. Nonetheless, he stepped off on the fifth floor and walked confidently down the hall. He stopped at a black glass door with a large Federal Bureau of Investigation Seal proudly displayed on it, then pulled the perfectly balanced door open and entered into the air conditioned silence of the government agency efficiently at work.

He walked over to the receptionist desk where an attractive white lady, wearing a designer business suit, a headset and a whisper-mic near her mouth worked diligently on a computer. She looked up and smiled at him when he neared the long and curved reception desk.

"May I help you?" she asked with a genuine smile.
"Yes, my name is Ron Perry and I'm here to meet with Agents Jeff McDonald and Steve Powaski."

"Oh, they are expecting you. You can go on down," she said pointing down the hallway to her right. "It will be the first door on your left."

Ron Perry smiled, then turned and walked toward the office. His apprehensions mounted as he got closer to the door. He wondered what the fuck they could want with him as stopped in front of the black door. Finally, he reached for the doorknob, gritted his teeth, turned the knob, pushed the door open and stepped inside.

Agents McDonald and Powaski stood up from their desks and walked over to Ron Perry and introduced themselves. They greeted him like old friends, but he knew better. They were the 'Feds' and there was nothing 'good' about the Feds…Especially for a crooked Philly cop.

Have a seat, Detective," Agent McDonald told Ron Perry.

Ron Perry sat down in an uncomfortable looking chair and waited for the worst. He could tell they were up to something. He just wondered what?

"So, let's get to it, shall we? What's this all about?" he asked, trying to look innocent and confused all at the same time. He folded his arms across his chest and waited.

"We invited you down here for something very important," Agent Powaski stated.

"And what's so important?" Ron Perry asked curiously.

"This man," Agent McDonald said, taking a large black and white photograph of Face out of a manila folder on his desk. "Norman 'Black Scarface' Smith, Junior. The new 'top man' in the city and our new number one target," he continued.

Ron Perry looked at both of the agents and said, "So, what do y'all need me for?"

Agent Powaski approached Ron Perry in a superior and semi aggressive manner and said, "Let's just cut the bullshit right now. We know all about you, Detective! All about you and Hood's drug organization. We know that you were once a major part of it and we also know how much you hate Face and his partner Reese Daniels. There's nothing that goes on in this city that we don't know about, Detective! Nothing!"

"So, what is it that I can do for you's?" Ron Perry smiled comfortably.

"We just need your help and all the information you have that can help us bring Face and Reese down for good. From our sources we have learned that the organization is supplied with drugs and weapons by two wealthy Nicaraguan brothers with powerful connections. For the past few years we have had our eyes on Face and his elaborate drug organization; watching them grow from a small crew of drug dealers to major cocaine and heroin wholesalers," Agent McDonald said.

Ron Perry laughed and said, "Then, y'all should know that for the past six years Face has built himself an unbreakable and untouchable drug organization. So far, he's been a mastermind

of modern day drug dealing and no one has been able to stop him."

"First of all, Detective Perry, he's neither unbreakable or untouchable and soon he will be stopped!" Agent Powaski stated angrily.

"Look here, I've been trying for six long years to bring Face and Reese down. And in those six years one State Prosecutor was murdered and so was four informants and too many witnesses to even start naming! You know what's worse? The cases we had against Face were all weak! The man has a spotless record! His wife owns one of the largest real estate firms in the country to account for all his wealth and they have one of the biggest non-profit charities in the Philadelphia and the South Jersey area. If the Feds plan to take down Face and his organization y'all better prepare for a real fight! And y'all better have substantial and irrefutable evidence and witnesses against him that can help y'all's case, otherwise y'all spinning y'alls wheels!" Ron Perry smiled factitiously. "Gentlemen, maybe y'all haven't realized it yet, but Norman 'Black Scarface' Smith Junior is in a league by himself," he added.

Agent McDonald grinned and said, "Detective have you ever heard the name C.W. Watson before?"

"No, enlighten me," Ron Perry smiled as if the name meant nothing but more police bungling.

"Well, Detective, earlier today Senator C.W. Watson was appointed by the President of the United States as the new head of the Domestic Anti-Drug Commission. Do you have any idea what that means?" McDonald asked.

"No, but I'm sure you're about to tell me," Ron Perry smirked nonchalantly.

"It means that we now have a man in power that's one hundred percent dedicated to winning this war on drugs. Tomorrow morning he will be at a conference in Washington, D.C. with the heads of the FBI, DEA, ATF, IRS and the Department of Homeland Security. Together they are about to establish a new National Organized Crime Task Force that's gonna be dedicated to bringing down the top people who supply the little ones with drugs. And you know what, Detective?"

"No, what?" Ron replied.

"BLACK SCARFACE is one of the many names on C.W. Watson's list of drug kingpins! So, Detective, are you with us, or against us?" McDonald asked, his eyes smoldering with

righteous fervor.

Ron Perry looked at both men and smiled. Then he stood up and said extending his hand, "Y'all can count me in!"

CHAPTER 80

Later that night...

The Belgravia, an upscale Center City condominium, on Chestnut Street, near 18th, was one of the places that Face and his family called home. Face and Tasha were sitting on the sofa talking and watching their children play on the carpet.

"So, how long will you be gone for this time, Face?" Tasha asked, as she ran her hand through his dark curly hair.

"Hopefully, just a few days. Don't worry I'll be back home before you know it," Face replied, enjoying Tasha's hand as she massaged his scalp.

"How was your private time at the house?"

"Very therapeutic. I had time to think. Which is always good."

Tasha looked at their children playing and said, "Time for bed y'all. Come give daddy a hug and kiss."

Norman III stood up, ran over and jumped into his father's lap. Norman III was their handsome five year old son and the spitting image of his father. Isuri their three year old beautiful baby daughter got up and joined her older brother, "Daddy! Daddy!" she said as she wrapped her little arm around his waist. Face gave each of them a kiss and hug and playfully tickled them. His family meant the world to him and his two young children were the jewels of his life.

"Okay, you two, come on," Miss. Elly said, standing a few feet away from the sofa. Miss. Elly was their live in maid and the children's personal caretaker. She was a black woman in her late 50s and she loved the children as if they were her very own. Other than immediate family, Miss. Elly was the only person that was allowed to be around them. Face didn't trust anyone else around his children.

After Miss. Elly took Norman III and Isuri to their bedroom, Face and Tasha retreated to their own room and closed the door. Tasha took off her silk robe and laid it across the arm of a chair. Then Face watched as she walked her naked body across the room and over to the bed.

"Okay, your turn," she said with a big grin. After all the years they had been together, Tasha was still very much attracted to his youthful and masculine handsomeness.

Every time she saw his naked and muscular physique she was in total awe. "Damn!" was all she could say.

After Face got undressed he joined her on the bed. They began kissing and moments later Tasha's moans filled the room. With her eyes tightly closed, her mind and body was somewhere between space and heaven.

* * *

For the past two and a half years Quincy now lived in Philly. Right after he was released from the San Quentin Prison, Face invited him to Philly to live and be a part of his crew. Quincy was Face's number one hitman and the leader of Face's own personal death squad.

In the two and a half years that Quincy lived in Philly, he had already killed eight men; one of them was a Philadelphia District Attorney. Standing at six feet three, Quincy had muscles popping out all over his tattooed body and he was an intimidating sight. The years he spent in prison had made him hard and bitter. He was a cold blooded killer who had no remorse for snitches, or the law. The only person that could control Quincy was Face, his younger brother, whom he loved more than anything else in life. There was nothing Quincy would not do for Face, even if it meant putting his own life on the line.

The black Cadillac Escalade pulled up on the corner of Chew and Chelten Avenue and Quincy rushed over and quickly got inside.

"What's up, Reese?" he said as they shook hands.

"Same ole' shit," Reese replied and he slowly pulled off. "You gotta hold the fort down tomorrow, while me and Face go out of town to take care of some business," he added.

"Don't worry, everything will be cool." Quincy looked at him. "You alright, Cuz?" he asked.

"Yeah, I'm cool. I just had a few things on my mind that's all."

"Like what? Spill it out," Quincy said.

When Reese stopped the truck at a red light he looked at Quincy and said, "My grandmother's birthday is in three days. I always get a little sad around this time of year."

Quincy knew the whole story about Reese's grandmother and his younger brother being killed inside their home. He could feel Reese's pain, because he had also experienced a similar

tragedy in his own life, when his mother and step father were murdered inside their bedroom. "I know just how you feel, Cuz. Hopefully time will heal some of your pain. Just don't bug out like you did last year," Quincy said, playfully pushing his shoulder.

The light turned green and Reese pulled off and said, "I'll try not to."

They were referring to an incident the year before when Reese got so drunk that he pissed all over himself and fainted. He had gotten so drunk that Quincy and Face had to carry him to his bed. Once there, he slept for twelve straight hours.

Thirty minutes later the truck pulled up in front of a small row house. Quincy said, "I'll see y'all in a few days. Don't worry everything will be cool while y'all gone." They gave each other a pound and Quincy got out of the truck.

When Reese pulled off, Quincy went inside the house. He walked straight up the stairs and entered into a back bedroom and immediately went to a closet that was filled with a plethora of weapons and ammunition. He had AK-47s, SKs, .9mm's, Uzi's, pump shotguns, .40 caliber Desert Eagles, silencers, a few bullet proof vests and so much more. Quincy was a gun fanatic, and at any given time he was prepared for an all out war.

Chestnut Hill, Philadelphia...

Veronica stood in her doorway as a tall white man got out of his car and rushed toward her. He was wearing a pair of dark shades and a short blond colored wig. Once inside, Veronica closed the door behind them. "Charles I don't like this!" she said, walking over to the stairs.

"Veronica, I'm the Mayor for God's sake! What do you expect?" he said following her up the stairs and into her bedroom. "I have a political career to protect. So, it's better to be safe than sorry," he told her.

Veronica stood in front of Charles and took off his shades and wig. "It just seems so childish. And you look so stupid," Veronica said as she tossed the shades and wig to the floor.

Charles picked Veronica up in his arms and said, "As long as I get to be with you. That's all that matters."

He laid her across the bed and watched as Veronica took off her robe. Seeing her beautiful naked body gave him an instant erection. Veronica gave him a seductive look as he started to get undressed. "You don't want to wait for Jeffery, Mr. Mayor?" she teased as she spread her legs wide apart. She watched as he removed a condom from its packet and unrolled it onto his dick. "I guess not," she smiled.

He walked over and eagerly joined his young black mistress on the bed. After all the years they had known each other, Charles, who was now the Mayor of Philadelphia, was still hooked on her sexual prowess, and he had no intentions of ever giving her up.

CHAPTER 81

Washington, D.C.

Early the next morning, 9:38 A.M...

Inside the J. Edgar Hoover Federal building a group of powerful, intelligent and political figures convened inside a large conference room. Ten men and two women sat around a large oval shaped conference table. They were all heads of federal agencies; FBI, ATF, DEA, U.S. Coast Guard, U.S. Treasury, Department of Homeland Security, the U.S. Attorney General and two senior members of the Senate.

Standing at the head of the table was Senator C.W. Watson, the new Presidentially appointed head of the Domestic Anti-Drug Commission. C.W. Wilson was a short stocky man with salt and pepper hair and light blue eyes. At five feet four inches tall, he was small in height, but he was a political giant. He established his powerful reputation as a member of in the Republican Party for the past thirty years. Where many respected him…many more feared him. C.W. Wilson was extremely serious about the new position the President entrusted him with and he was determined to clean up America's violent streets and finally win the loosing war on drugs.

But behind closed doors, a few powerful men knew that C.W. Watson's new position was only a stepping stone for something much bigger. In the next two years, if all went well, C.W. Watson would be the next Republican candidate for the United States Presidency.

"Ladies and Gentlemen, we have a very serious crisis on our hands!" C.W. said, as his piercing blue eyes scanned the room. "And I was appointed to clean things up," he added.

There was a collective sigh from around the table as others agreed with him.

"My first task is to go right after the big boys. The so called, 'kingpins'! And all the drug smugglers that bring their garbage into our country."

C.W. opened his brown folder and took out a small stack of paper. He walked around the table and passed one sheet to each person.

"I want all of you to look very closely at the names and faces of the people on that page." Everyone did as he asked. "The men that you are looking at are the top five drug dealers in America. Ladies and Gentlemen, in the next two years I want every man on that list to be brought to justice! And I will use everything in my power to personally bring each one of these men down!

Everyone on The Anti-Drug Commission Committee started clapping and nodding their heads in agreement. "We will no longer stand for our great country to be run by low life scum of the earth! It's time to take back control of our country and I'm the man that was appointed the job to do it!" he wholeheartedly declared.

Once again all the committee members attending the private conference erupted in applause and enthusiastically nodded their heads in agreement.

After the meeting ended, C.W. Watson and another man was escorted outside and lead to an awaiting black limousine. They climbed inside and closed the doors.

"That was a good speech. I think you made your point," the man said.

"Thanks Robert because I meant every word I said. And I won't let anything stop me from getting in the White House. Nothing!" C.W. stated.

"How about we fly down to my property in South Carolina and do a little hunting this weekend? It's been a while," Robert said changing the subject.

"That sounds like a good idea. I have a Senate meeting tomorrow morning, but afterward you can count me in", C.W. said with a smile. Then he reached over and grabbed the phone.

Ibiza, a small island in the Mediterranean, off the coast of Valencia, Spain...

On the north side of the exotic island the clear blue water surrounded the sixty foot yacht. The yacht was far enough away from the island's shore that complete privacy was not an issue. Six men stood out on the large deck talking and enjoying the beautiful weather. There was Rico and Jose Gomez, their top man Roberto Chevez, Face, Reese and a dark skinned, stocky man named Lance.

Lance was a drug kingpin from Cleveland, Ohio who the Gomez brothers supplied with 1500 to 2000 kilos a month.

"Anyway Face, like I was saying, my friend, we don't have anything to worry about. This guy C.W. Watson is just another front man that's been appointed to fool the public," Rico said.

Face nodded his head and took a sip of his French wine.

"So what do you think of all of this, Lance, you've been pretty quiet all morning," Rico asked.

"Huh?" Lance said, snapping out of his daze.

"I said, what do you think of all this talk about this new guy C.W. Watson? The head of the Domestic Anti-Drug Commission," Rico asked again.

"Uhm...I don't...I don't know nothing about him," Lance answered nervously.

Everyone looked at Lance with suspicious eyes. Since coming to the island he had been a nervous wreck. But the Gomez brothers told him it was imperative that he be there for a very important meeting. Both Face and Reese wondered why Lance was there. It was the first time the Gomez's had ever invited someone else to one of their meetings. It was something that Face had always opposed. He knew that the less people who knew his name and saw his face the better.

Rico walked over to Jose and Roberto and whispered something into each of their ears.

"Face do you and Reese mind standing over there? Jose asked, pointing near the end of the deck.

Face and Reese did as they were asked and wondered what was going on.

Lance stood there looking fearful and uneasy about his current situation. Sweat involuntarily poured from his forehead and it wasn't from the hot scorching sun.

Face and Reese stood back and watched as all three men surrounded Lance. Suddenly all three of them pulled their guns out from under their shirts. Lance's eyes widened in total fear.

"What the hell is..."

"Shut the fuck up and take off all your clothes!" Rico said, cutting him off in mid sentence.

Lance knew they were serious and started taking off all of his clothes.

Face and Reese watched everything from a short distance.

After Lance had taken off all his clothes he stood there totally naked and fearfully asked, "please Rico, what's this all about?"

Rico reached down and picked up his tropical colored shorts and slid the black leather belt out of the belt loops. He closely examined the strange looking square shaped buckle. Then

raised it up high in the air and smashed it hard against the teakwood deck of the yacht. When the buckle cracked open several small electrical components bounced and rolled across the deck exposing the well disguised recording device.

"So Lance, what agency made the belt for you... FBI? DEA? Who?! You fucking snitch!" Rico shouted.

"We found out everything!" Jose said. "We know all about the Feds catching you with drugs and weapons," he added.

Lance stood there speechless. His trembling body was covered in sweat.

"Do you know what we do to snitches and informants who work for the government? Motherfuckers like you who try to take us down?!" Rico vented.

"Please, man!" Lance begged with eyes filled with tears and fear.

Rico shook his head in disgust. Then, he, Jose and Roberto aimed and squeezed the triggers of their loaded Berretta .9mm's, sending bullets into Lance's head and body. They watched as his dead, shot up body dropped hard on the deck's surface.

Together they picked up Lance's corpse and tossed it over the side of the yacht and into the warm Mediterranean sea.

Rico walked over to Face and Reese, "There's nothing I hate more than a snitch!" he said before walking down the stairs.

CHAPTER 82

Two days later inside a safe-house in West Oak Lane, Philadelphia...

When Face and Reese returned from their trip Quincy had everything running smoothly. While they were away he made sure everything was under control and money kept pouring in. Quincy passed Face a back pack filled with cash. "That's two hundred and fifty thousand dollars," he said. "I'm running over to Jersey tomorrow to pick up the rest," he added.

"Good job, Quincy," Face said, as he looked across the table at Reese.

Reese was sitting at the table daydreaming. For the past few days he had been in a somber mood and sorrow was written all over his face.

"Reese! Yo Reese!" Face said smacking the table.

Reese jerked his head and woke up from his day dream. When he looked across at the table Face and Quincy were both staring at him.

"Is you alright, man?" Face asked caringly. "'Cause you been really out of it the last few days," he added.

"Yeah, I'm cool, man. Just had some shit on my mind, that's all," Reese said, standing up from his chair.

Face already knew what Reese's problem was because he too was dealing with the pain of losing Momma and D.J.; Face was just better at hiding his emotions.

"Face, I got some thinking to do. How 'bout y'all handle this without me tonight and I'll get with y'all tomorrow?" Reese said with a grim tone.

"You sure?"

"Yeah, I just need to drive around and clear my mind a little," Reese replied.

"Okay, just be safe. Luv you."

"Love you, too. See you tomorrow," Reese stated as he turned around and walked out of the living room.

When Reese had left the house, Quincy looked at Face and said, "He's going through it, man! I understand his pain, Face. I had to go through that same fucked up feeling when

my mom and stepfather got killed."

"I understand Quincy, but you got over it and moved on. Reese is letting Momma's death bring him down. And that's not good for a man in his position. I'm hurting too. Momma was like my grandmother and D.J. was like my little brother. But, I knew that if I didn't accept it and move on, that it would likely kill me. And that's what it's doing to Reese," Face said.

"We have a multi-million dollar a month drug business going on and I need my right hand man to be focused at all times, he added.

Sitting inside his black Cadillac Escalade, Reese reached over, opened the glove compartment and took out the small photos. He sat there staring at the pictures of Momma and D.J. with watery eyes. Not a day had gone by without him thinking about both of them. Many times he had blamed himself for their murders.

As the flow of tears fell down his face, Reese put the photos back, closed the glove compartment then reached under his seat and grabbed a bottle of Hennessey. Tearfully, he

unscrewed the top and raised the bottle up to his mouth, "I love you, Momma. Happy Birthday!"

After swallowing a big gulp, he sat the bottle between his thighs. When his cell phone started ringing he looked on the small caller ID screen and saw that it was from his fiancée.

Passion had been worried about him and had called him repeatedly for the last hour.

Reese put his cell phone down on the passenger seat, then started up his truck. As tears continued to fall as he pulled off and drove down the street. Every few minutes he would put the bottle to his lips and swallow another big gulp. As he drove to nowhere in particular, he cried, grieved and continued to drink away his pain.

* * *

Inside the T&F offices, Tasha and Pamela were sitting around talking about a new property acquisition, when Passion sadly walked back into the office.

"Girl, you still ain't get in touch with Reese?" Pamela asked.

"No, Ms. Pam, he still ain't answering his cell phone. And I'm afraid...afraid...that..."

"Afraid of what? Tasha asked as she closed a black briefcase.

"I'm afraid that Reese will do something crazy today. Just like he did last year when he got drunk and started acting like a mad man," Passion replied.

"Just keep trying to call him. He'll eventually answer. Today's Momma's birthday. He's just hurting. But, sooner or later, he'll come around," Pamela said with compassion.

"I sure hope so," Passion said, sitting down in a chair. Tasha and Pamela watched as Passion started rubbing around her round plump belly. Passion was five months pregnant.

She and Reese were expecting their first child.

"Girl, you don't need to be stressing over nonsense. That ain't good for the baby," Tasha said in a caring voice.

"She's right, Passion. Stressing will only make matters worse," Pamela agreed.

As they sat there talking, a tall attractive white woman opened the door, and stuck her head inside. "Mrs. Smith, your meeting with the Chinese investors will start in five minutes.

They are all in the main conference room," she said.

"Thanks Amber. Come on Miss Pam, let's go get ready," Tasha said, then she and Pamela grabbed their briefcases and rushed out the office.

When Pamela and Tasha left Amber closed the office door behind them, then she sat down in a empty seat beside Passion.

Amber 'White Chocolate' Kennedy, looked into her best friend's worried eyes and said, "Passion don't worry. Reese will be all right. He just needs a little time and space."

As her eyes began to water, Passion looked at Amber and said, "I hope so, but, something just don't feel right!"

On the corner of 9th and Walnut Street...

A tinted black Ford Taurus was parked behind a brand new grey colored Yukon Danali truck. Agent McDonald and Powaski sat up front while Detective Ron Perry sat on the back seat.

Ron Perry passed Agent McDonald a thick brown folder and said, "That's all the information that I've gathered on Face and Reese in the last six years. The majority of the stuff is miscellaneous; school records, car payments and so on. But there's a few photos. Like I said, most of the information I've gathered over the years is all miscellaneous. That's why I've never been able to build a strong enough case against them. Their circle has been too strong to crack, and the few witnesses we did have all ended up dead including the D.A. that got killed a few years back. The same one that was assigned to their case by the State."

"Don't worry Ron, we'll go through everything you got here and see what we can use. Right now we don't have anything solid or strong enough to bring them down. But, that won't last long! When the government wants somebody, we'll do everything in our power to get'em!" Agent Powaski added with a smile.

"Alright, I'll call you if I find out anything new," Ron Perry said. He shook both men's hands and got out of the car. They watched as Ron Perry walked over to his Denali truck and climbed inside. When he pulled off down the street, they drove off right behind him.

West Philadelphia...

Reese slowly pulled his truck up at the red light and stopped. One hand gripped the steering wheel while the other hand tightly clutched the half empty bottle of Hennesy. In a drunken state he sat back crying and listening to his favorite hard core street rapper, 50 Cent. Reese was filled with anguish and his soul cried out to his murdered grandmother and younger brother. Suddenly, the red light switched colors and Reese pressed hard on the gas pedal.

The black Escalade truck sped off down the street. "Momma!" Reese cried out. "Momma! Momma!" he shouted as 50 Cent's hardcore lyrics and pulsating beats banged out of the truck's 18 inch woofers. As the large black truck sped recklessly down the street, Reese never noticed the young teenage girl walking across the street. When he finally looked up, it was too late.

BOOMPPP!!!

The truck smashed right into the girl's small frame. Her body flew about twenty feet into the air and landed on top of a parked car. Reese tried his best to control his vehicle, but the truck ended up crashing head on into a wooden street light pole. The hard impact propelled Reese and sent him flying straight through the shattered front glass window, knocking him totally unconscious.

As for the young fourteen year old girl, on her way home from school…she was less fortunate. With a cracked skull and broken neck, she never had a chance.

One hour later, Downtown Philadelphia...

Inside his lawyer's lush office, Face sat across from his desk reviewing the financial records of his off shore accounts in the Cayman Islands, and the Atlantic International Bank in Belize. His high powered lawyer and financial advisor, Peter J. Greenberg, smiled proudly as he sat behind his desk with his arms folded across his chest.

Peter came highly recommended by Face's good friend Veronica, and for three years he had been Face's personal lawyer and financial advisor/consultant. Together they were creating a financial empire.

Peter was a financial whiz; a former Wall Street investor who had worked for Merrill Lynch, and was once head of the investment banking division.

"How's it look," Peter asked.

"As good as always," Face replied, then passed the papers back to Peter.

"You're making twenty one percent on your money…every year!

One hell of a return," Peter stated. "The great thing about it Face, is that it is completely untouchable and untraceable, just like I promised you," he added.

"Peter, you're the man!" Face said excitedly.

"No Face, you're the man. That was a very smart idea, never putting anything in your name. And to let your wife purchase all of your personal assets under the company name. The less of a paper trail, the better," Peter said, in a stern tone.

"At the rate you're going, you'll be a billionaire before you know it," he added.

Feeling his cell phone vibration on his hip, Face reached down and grabbed it. He looked at the caller ID and quickly answered, "What's up, Mom?"

It's Reese, Face. Reese is in the hospital. He just had a bad car accident!" Pamela said excitedly.

"What? Is he okay?" Face asked apprehensively.

"I think so. But, he's pretty banged up. He was drunk when it happened."

"Where is he? " Face asked.

"He's at Presbyterian Hospital."

"I'm on my way!" Face told her.

"Baby, there's more," Pamela said.

"What else is it?"

After a long sigh, Pamela said, "Reese hit a fourteen year old girl and she died at the scene."

"I'm on my way!" Face said, closing the cell phone and rushing out of Peter's office.

CHAPTER 83

Late May, three weeks later...

After being released from the hospital with minor head injuries, bruised ribs and a broken collar bone, Reese was immediately taken into police custody and charged with vehicular homicide in the death of the 14 year old girl.

Face hired a high powered attorney named, James Black, to represent him at the upcoming trial. Using his powerful connections, James Black was able to get the vehicular homicide dropped to a much lesser offense, vehicular manslaughter. But, even with the success of the first charge being dropped to a lesser charge, Reese would still have to serve some time away in state prison and there was nothing anyone could do to stop it.

Inside the county jail, Face, Reese and his attorney James Black, sat on a bench inside a half crowded visiting room.

"So, how much time is they talking about?" Reese asked his lawyer.

After a sigh, James said, "At least six years. If all goes well, you could be out in four."

"Six fucking years!" Reese protested angrily. "My girl is about to have our first child! When I get out my baby won't even know me!" he added, looking to Face for help and understanding.

"Reese, because of the negative press you got and all the heat from the M.A.D.D. organization, that's the best I could do. Remember, you were intoxicated and you took a young girl's life. Whether it was accidental or not, the public doesn't care. It could be a whole lot worse," James said."You're getting a break and everyone knows it," he added.

Face looked at Reese and just shook his head. Since the accident, he had been more disappointed in Reese, and now with his callus reaction to the young girl's death, he was more disappointed than ever.

"Face, I'm sorry man," Reese said apologetically. "It was all my fault and I deserve everything that happening to me. Fuck!" he added, accepting the realization of what awaited him.

Face reached over and placed his hand on Reese's shoulder and squeezed it tightly, reassuringly, then said, "I'm very disappointed in you, Reese, but I'll get over it. You're my

brother and partner."

Reese's eyes watered as they gave each other a brotherly hug. "Did you take care of that for me?" Reese asked.

"Yeah, I had Tasha write out a check for a million dollars and deliver it to the family with your deepest apologies for their loss and your request for their forgiveness."

"Thanks Face, I really appreciate that," Reese said honestly, then looked straight into Face's eyes and said, "So, will you be able to handle things without me for a little while?"

"I'll manage, but it won't be the same. I'll have to fight this war with my left hand," he frowned.

"Why's that?" Reese asked with a look of confusion.
"Because, my right hand is going off to prison," he answered.

Reese watched as Face and James Black stood up from their seats. Even though he was handcuffed to the edge of the table, Reese stood also. His fluorescent orange jumpsuit seemed to

glow as more of it was exposed when he stood.

"I have an early morning meeting with the Prosecutor. I'll inform him that we're accepting his offer," James told Reese.

"I'll see you soon," he added, as he shook their hands, then turned, walked through the visiting room and disappeared through a door at the other end of the hall.

Face and Reese gave each other another long hug, "Just go do your time and hurry back home. All your money will be safely put away. And don't worry about Passion and your baby.

They won't need or want for anything, I promise... nor will you while you're away."

"Thanks Face," Reese said softly.

After visiting hours were over, Reese and a long line of other inmates were escorted back to their cells.

When Face got into his Mercedes he sat there for a few moments staring straight ahead into the distance. His mind was clouded and raced with thoughts as he contemplated the future without Reese. As tears fell down his cheeks he started the car and slowly drove off.

Parked a few cars away, four cold calculating eyes watched from the tinted windows of a Ford Taurus as Face drove away. "It ain't what we wanted, but I'll take it," Agent McDonald stated.

"Still, that's one down and one more to go," Agent Powaski said with a laugh. "Now, we can put all of our efforts, time and resources into bringing Face down!" he gleefully added as they pulled out of the parking spot and headed downtown to their office on 6th street.

Two days later, East Hampton, Long Island, New York...

After Face's meeting with Quincy and all of his top street lieutenants he decided to leave town and go clear his head. A lot was on his mind and Reese's current imprisonment

only made matters worse.

Inside his elegant Hampton estate, Face sat on the sofa watching CNN. Laying beside him were the New York Times and the Wall Street Journal that he just finished reading. The tranquility of the mansion home gave Face the solitude that he needed to put his many thoughts together. He sat back focused on the TV as the house servants walked about doing their jobs. They all knew not to disturb him and were trying their best to comply with his orders and wishes. Nonetheless, everyone understood that the servants had jobs to do, so they worked around him.

He grabbed the remote control to turn the TV off but, just before he pressed the off button a beautiful black face appeared in the top right corner of the screen. He quickly turned the volume up and got more relaxed on the sofa as he listened intently. A curious expression appeared on his face as he sat back watched and listened in disbelief.

"Earlier today, in the Manhattan Federal Courthouse, alleged 'Mob Boss', Vincent Maletto was acquitted of all charges," the news anchor read from the teleprompter with no emotion. "He's the first 'Mob Boss' in the past twenty years to get indicted twice by a Federal Grand Jury on racketeering charges and was acquitted both times. In both trials, Mr. Maletto was represented by Defense Attorney, Gloria Jones Henderson, wife of State Representative Robert L. Henderson..."

"Gloria?" Face whispered, turning the volume back down and then turning the set off. Then he laid his head back on the sofa and repeatedly whispered her name, remembering the times they had shared. Truthfully, he hadn't thought of her for several years. She had promised that one day she would become the top criminal defense attorney in the nation, and she had done it. Not only had she made a name for herself as a successful advocate, but she had also gotten married. Face was proud of her. As he laid back, he closed his eyes and a big smile was plastered across his face.

September 5, 2006...

Passion had given birth to a seven pound eight ounce baby girl. She and Reese named her Amiaya 'Lilly' Daniels. A few weeks later, Passion and Reese got married inside the prison's chapel at S.C.I. Graterford, in upstate Pennsylvania. Reese's designated prison term was for at least the next four years. Passion was determined to stick by her husband's side through thick and thin and so far, she had yet to miss a single visit.

Face had also visited Reese a few times, keeping him up to date with everything that was going on with the drug business. He also made sure Reese's commissary account stayed full and

that his mind stayed sharp and focused with some of the self-help books he sent him.

As far as trouble from other inmates at the prison, there was nothing to worry about. Before Reese went to the Graterford compound, Face contacted his friends on the inside and told them to take good care of Reese and make sure his time at the prison went smooth and problem free.

In the meantime, Face and the Gomez brothers were moving tons of cocaine and heroin throughout the country. They had added more major cities to their list; New Orleans, Cincinnati, Ohio and Richmond, Virginia.

For a three week long period, Face had made a million and a half dollars a day. Money was pouring in by the boatloads. Now Face had to meet with his attorney and financial advisor, Peter J. Greenberg, twice a week to keep it all moving and inaccessible.

CHAPTER 84

Washington, D.C., April 15, seven months later...

Inside the elegant five-star French restaurant, C.W. Watson and Tom Klein, his best friend for more than forty years, watched their wives as they excused themselves and went to the Ladies room. Tom, a self-made millionaire and businessman from Scranton, Pennsylvania was also the father of Charles Klein, the current Mayor of Philadelphia. They proudly watched the women walk away, then Tom turned his attention to C.W. and said, "So, C.W., you've been all over the news lately. How's everything going?" He sipped his expensive French Bordeaux and waited for an answer.

"Everything is going well since I was appointed to head of the Domestic Anti-Drug Commission. There have been ten major drug busts from all around the country. In fact there is a

major undercover 'sting' operation that's going down in the next few days," C.W. proudly replied. "A big one," he added with emphasis.

"So, is it true…this job is a stepping stone to the Oval Office?" Tom asked, sipping his wine and knowing his friend wouldn't lie to him.

"I believe so. I have a lot of powerful supporters backing me; including the current President," C.W. said with a sly grin.

"Then you should be a shoo in?" Tom stated, convinced.

"We'll see," C.W. replied, as he reached for his wine flute. Like the connoisseur he was, he gently swiveled the wine in its glass and sniffed it, before tasting and savoring the robust flavors of the five hundred dollar bottle of wine.

After which, C.W. looked at Tom and asked, "so, how's my Godson doing in his new job?"

I talked with Charles yesterday. He says he loves being the Mayor in Philly."

"Good, I'm proud of him. Think we can ever persuade Charles to go hunting with us again?" C.W asked with a knowing grin.

Tom laughed and said, "I doubt it, not after what happened the last time. He hasn't been hunting since."

"Do you think Charles got over it? It's been over thirty years. "

"He was a kid back then and used to have nightmares about it. But, as he got older, the nightmares began to fade. I'm sure he's fine now," Tom replied reassuringly.

When their wives returned to the table, C.W. and Tom quickly changed the subject.

Belmopan. Belize...

The Atlantic International Bank had assets worth over 3.8 billion dollars. Anyone that wanted to be completely discrete with their money opened accounts there. It was one of the last tax shelters that hadn't opened their books to the United States government. So many wealthy people took advantage of the opportunity and used the bank to hide their money. It didn't matter what your profession was-if you had the five million dollar minimum, you could open account and your money would be deposited.

Face and his lawyer Peter J. Greenberg walked out of the bank and got inside a tinted black limousine. Face had just deposited another twenty million dollars into his account.

The limo slowly pulled off.

"What do you plan to do with all that money?" Peter asked.

"Use it to make more. The more money I have, the more powerful I become.," Face replied seriously. "One day I would like to build a legacy like the Kennedys or the Rockafellers or Gates'," he added.

Peter looked at his young friend and smiled. "At the rate you're going, that won't be hard at all," he said.

Forty minutes later the limousine pulled into a hangar at the Belize International Airport. Waiting for them inside, was the Gomez brother's 5.7 million dollar Beechcraft Permere

1 jet. Face and Peter got out of the limousine, walked over and boarded the six-seater jet.

"I have a meeting at three o'clock in my office. Do you think we'll be back in Philly in time?"

Face looked down at his Patek Philippe watch and smiled as he looked at Peter and said, "You'll be there an hour before your meeting starts."

Two days later, Laredo, Texas...

Roberto Chevez stood, watching as seven of his Mexican workers unloaded the large eighteen wheeler truck. The cargo was Columbia's finest export; kilos of pure cocaine. Over five tons of it were stacked neatly inside.

Roberto had just gotten off the phone with Rico Gomez and told him know that all four shipments had made it from across the Mexican border. Also inside the trailer was five hundred kilos of Afghani born heroin, all safely packaged and ready to flood the streets of urban America.

"Hurry! Hurry!" Roberto said, looking at his gold Rolex timepiece. He had to be back in Miami by nightfall, where another major shipment would be coming through. But as he stood there yelling at his workers to speed up the pace, the entire property was quickly surrounded by U.S. Government agents and local law enforcement officers. Roberto had no idea that his four armed bodyguards outside had already been apprehended. The takedown had been so quiet and swift that they didn't know what had hit them.

For two weeks the Feds had the entire property under surveillance. They knew times, dates and places of every new drug shipment, Roberto Chevez was smuggling and planning to smuggle into America. Unbeknownst to Roberto Chevez, he was one of the top domestic and international drug dealers on C.W. Watson's list of major drug suspects. While Roberto continued to yell at his workers armed Federal Agents and members of the local police department approached and blocked all exits and entrances to the large barn.

Suddenly, all the doors of the barn were crashed in and armed FBI, DEA, ATF and members of the local Sheriff's department came pouring in and brandishing their loaded weapons.

"FBI! FBI! Get on the ground, now!" an approaching agent shouted. His short assault weapon was leveled at Roberto's chest and that of his workers. Roberto and all of his workers quickly threw up their hands, each one of them had an expression of total disbelief.

"Get on the ground, NOW!" the agent shouted again, raising the barrel to point at Roberto's head. Roberto quickly did as he was told. His workers not understanding English, followed his lead and placed their hands on the back of their heads interlacing their fingers.

A feeling of absolute fear and helplessness swept through Roberto's body. He could not believe that he had been busted. After all the years he had been working for the Gomez brothers

it was the first time he had ever been caught. The worst part of it all was the shipment that had just come through, was the largest shipment ever!

Roberto lay on the ground shaking his head and mumbling words under his breath. He looked around watching as agents seized all of the drugs and sealed off the area with yellow

crime scene tape. Then, he watched as one by one, his seven scared workers were handcuffed, lifted from the ground and escorted outside. Roberto was the last man left. He lay there

wondering what was going on, when a tall, white FBI agent approached and said, "Okay, Mr. Chevez, you can get up now."

Roberto slowly stood up and looked around confused, then he looked into the agent's stern eyes. Another agent pulled Roberto's hands behind his back and handcuffed his wrists.

"My name is Special Agent Eric Grey. You'll be going with me." he said, taking Robert's arm and gently and leading him out of the barn. Outside a black FBI helicopter was waiting, it's rotor spun quickly, but gently, as the engine idled patiently. As they boarded, the rotor began to speed up and as they buckled into their seats, the chopper lifted from the ground, nose down, then spun around and roared into the distant sky.

"Roberto's mind was spinning and he was confused with the suddenness of his arrest. "What…what…what's going on?" He finally said, absolutely terrified.

Agent Grey looked over at Roberto and smiled evilly, "You're in a lot of trouble, Mr. Chevez," he said then he looked back out his window and ignored Roberto. He knew it was better to allow the prisoner to stew in his own imagination and fear rather than to try an intimidate him into talking. He had all the time in the world.

Later that evening, Chestnut Hill, , Philadelphia…

The older white man sat on the edge of Veronica's bed watching as she slowly stripped off all of her clothing. When she was completely naked, he stared in lustful awe as she performed an intoxicating and seductive dance that was meant to drive him to the edge. He was hard and excited with anticipation and could hardly wait to be deep inside of her warm, wet pussy.

Veronica grooved her way over to him and got down on her knees in front of him, then reached out and grabbed his throbbing dick with one hand. She looked down at it, then her big, lust filled eyes, slowly looked up at him. "Are you ready, Anthony?" she teased.

He nodded his head and whispered, "Yes".

"What time do you have to be back home to your wife?" she asked while she slowly and softly kissed around the head of his dick.

"She's out of town and since I don't have any cases today, I'm all yours," he said with a lustful, excited grin.

"Good," Veronica whispered softly. Then in one smooth motion, she slid Anthony's dick into her mouth and watched as his eyes found a wonderful place in the back of his head. She

smiled because her seductive acting ability was once again being caught on digital tape, so she gave Judge Anthony T. Marino the best blowjob of his life.

Northeast Philadelphia...

Inside his bedroom, Lil' Robbie sat on the edge of his bed. He reached under his pillow and took out a few small photographs. They were photos of his deceased parents. Not a day had gone by that Robbie didn't think about them, and the person that was responsible for their deaths; his older brother, Face.

In the quietness of his bedroom Robbie stared down into the photos. Streams of tears fell from his brown eyes and rolled down his cheeks. The gentle knock on his door startled him and snapped him out of his momentary daze.

"Come in," he said, already knowing who it was.

The door slowly opened and his fifteen year old sister Arianna walked inside. Arianna was growing up to be a tall and beautiful young woman. She had long curly black hair, a light caramel complexion and piercing green eyes, just like her mother. The boys at her high school constantly vied for her attention and Robbie constantly threatened and chased them away.

Arianna sat on the edge of the bed beside her brother and looked into his watery eyes. She loved her brother more than anything else in life and she knew Robbie felt the same way about her. They were as close as siblings could be.

"You all right?" she asked in a caring voice.

"Yeah, just sitting here thinking about Mom and Dad," Robbie replied, wiping his tears away with his hand. He looked deep into Arianna's eyes and said, "One day I'ma get all the people who was responsible for killing our parents."

"Just remember what daddy used to always tell us; that the more education we get, the more power we'll have." she replied.

"I just want them dead!" Robbie vented. "And I don't care how long it takes! I'ma get them all!"

Arianna grabbed both of Robbie's hands and said, "We're gonna get them all! But, we have to be smart about it, Robbie!"

Arianna gave Robbie a soft kiss on the cheek, then stood up from the bed and walked over to the door. Before she left out the room she paused and turned around. "Don't worry, big brother, one day we're gonna make Mommy and Daddy proud." She said, then left the room.

CHAPTER 85

Inside their condominium...

Tasha and Pamela sat on the sofa watching as Face and Norman III playfully wrestled on the soft carpet. Ms. Elly was sitting on another chair braiding Isuri's hair.

"Get him, Daddy!" Isuri shouted out.

Norman III had his father lying on his a back and pinned on the floor.

"You win! You win!" Face said.

Norman III got off his father and raised his arms into the air. "I'm the champion!" he said excitedly. Then he ran over to Pamela and gave her a big hug. "Grandma, I won!" he said.

"Yes, you did, Baby," Pamela agreed with a big smile.

"Daddy let you win," Isuri said. "Didn't you, Daddy?"

"No, he beat me fair and square," Face said, as he smiled and winked an eye at her.

When Face heard his cell phone ring he stood up from the floor and walked over to the table. He knew that it could only be one of three people; Roberto, Rico or Jose Gomez. No one else had his private number.

When Face approached the table he picked up the cell phone and looked at the caller ID. When he saw who it was he quickly answered.

"What's up? I wasn't expecting to hear from you for a few more days," Face said.

"Well a few things came up, so I decided to call you, now," Roberto said.

"Is everything alright? You don't sound like your regular self," Face said, as he sat down in one of the chairs.

"Yeah, everything is fine," Roberto replied.

"Okay then, what's up? Talk to me," Face replied.

"Tomorrow morning your next shipment will be ready. All 2500 will be waiting for you at the house. Plus, another 250 pounds of brown sugar," Roberto said, using the code name they

used for heroin.

"Alright. What time do you want me to swing by and pick up my groceries?" Face asked.

"Around eight-thirty. I'll meet you at the house."

"Are you okay" Face asked once again.

"I'm fine. I'll see you in the morning. Just be there on time," Roberto said, before he hung up the phone.

When the line went dead, Face closed his cell phone and sat back bemused. His intuition was telling him something was wrong.

Washington, D.C...

Special Agent Eric Gray reached over and turned off the phone recorder. It was the third and final recorded phone conversation that Roberto had made for him.

"You did good, Roberto. And like I promised, you'll be placed inside the Witness Protection Program and safe from all harm. Once we get everyone, we won't need you again until the trial," he said.

Roberto sat across from Agent Gray nodding his head. He felt bad about what he had just done; setting up another close friend for the federal government. Roberto had flipped sides

and was now working with the Feds and became their number one witness against Face and the Gomez brothers. For Roberto it was the only chance he had to escape a life sentence inside

a federal prison.

Agent Gray stood from his chair and said, "I have to notify our agents in Philly and tell them to be ready for tomorrow morning."

Roberto watched as he took out the small cassette tape and put it in his shirt pocket. "We now have Norman 'Face' Smith, Jr., one of the biggest drug dealers in the country on tape conspiring to purchase twenty five hundred kilos of cocaine and two hundred and fifty kilos of heroin. After he's busted tomorrow morning, his life sentence will be inevitable!" Agent Gray said with excitement.

Roberto put his head down in total disgust. For over five hours he told the Feds everything they had wanted to know about Face and the Gomez brothers. The only thing he didn't tell them about was all the murders they had committed through the years and, some of which he had been personally involved in.

After two agents escorted Roberto out of the room, Agent Gary had some very important phone calls to make.

Manhattan, New York...

Inside their luxurious condominium at the Chelsa House complex, Rico and Jose had just learned some disturbing news from one of their top men in Miami. They had just found out that Roberto had been busted down in Texas. And he never showed up in Miami. What was more disturbing was the fact that Roberto had called them an hour earlier as if everything was all right, and he didn't mention anything about being arrested.

Jose watched as Rico paced the living room floor. "He set us up! Roberto is now working for the Feds. And now he has our conversation on tape!" Rico fumed. "We have

to get out of the country. The Feds will be coming for us real soon," he added.

Jose took out his cell phone and quickly dialed a number.

"Who're you calling?" Rico asked.

"Face, I gotta let him know what's going on," Jose replied.

After the third ring Face answered his phone, "Yo, what's up?" he said.

"Face, Roberto was busted by the Feds this morning in Texas. If he calls you, don't answer your phone. We believe he's working with the Feds, trying to set us all up!" Jose said

in a somber tone.

"What? I just got off the phone with Roberto. He called me and told me about the new shipment that's coming through tomorrow," Face said.

"Don't go! It's a set-up! And another thing, do yourself a big favor and get out of town as soon as possible. I'll call you back in a few days," Jose said, before ending the call and

dialing another number.

After Jose made the phone call he looked at Rico and said, "Our limo is waiting out front. We need to get to our plane as soon as possible. The safest place for us is any where far away from American soil."

With worried expressions, Rico and Jose both rushed out the front door. They got into an awaiting elevator and Rico pressed the 'Lobby' button, then stood back as the doors closed and the elevator began to slowly descend.

Outside their building, at the corner of 130 West and 19th Street, two tinted, all black Ford Explorers were parked and armed with Federal Agents waiting inside both trucks. One agent in the truck, read over their arrest warrants. They knew the Gomez brothers would try to leave the country and they weren't going to allow that to happen.

They watched as the Gomez brothers exited the building and quickly climbed inside their waiting limousine.

"Let's take them down!" one of the agents said.

The two Ford Explorers sped off down the street and stopped in front of the limousine.

Rico and Jose sat on the back seat watching as armed FBI agents rushed out of the trucks and surrounded the limousine.

"Fuck!" Rico yelled angrily.

"Get out of the car, now! an agent shouted. His loaded .9mm pistol was pointed at the back window.

The back door opened and the two brothers slowly stepped outside.

"Yes, how can we help you?" Jose calmly said.

"You are both being placed under arrest for committing and conspiring to commit crimes against the United States Government. That's all I can tell you right now. You have the right to

remain silent." the agent continued to read them their Miranda Rights as another two agents handcuffed them and their driver. They were then escorted to the Explorers, Rico to one

and Jose to the other. Several other agents began going through the inside of the limo, looking for evidence to use against them.

When they were settled inside, the Explorers sped off and drove down the dark street.

The Agent then took out his cell phone and dialed a number.

"Hello?" a male voice answered.

"Agent Gray, this is agent Peterson. The two suspects have been apprehended. They are on their way to D.C. now," he said into the phone.

"Good job," Agent Gray said happily, then hung up the phone.

Philadelphia, Pa...

Face walked into the living room and said, "Miss. Elly, can you get the kids ready for bed. I need to talk with my wife and mother."

"Okay kids, y'all heard your father. Let's go get ready for bed," she told them.

Norman III and Isuri both walked over and gave their father a kiss and a hug. After they did the same to their mother and grandmother, Ms Elly escorted them towards the back bedroom.

"What's wrong Face?" Pamela asked, seeing his worried expression.

Tasha noticed it also, and said, "Face is everything all right?"

Face stared at both of the women and said, "I think I'm in a lot of trouble! One of my friends got busted this morning and I think he's now working with the Feds to try and set me

up."

"What!?" Tasha exclaimed in surprise.

"I have to hurry up and get out of town. The Feds will be here looking for me," Face replied.

"Where will you go?" Pamela asked, as tears started to well up in her eyes.

"I'm going to the house in New York. No one knows about that house. Not even the Feds. I need some time to focus and to get my thoughts in order."

Tasha walked over and gave Face a long, loving, hug. "Baby, just tell me what you need for me to do for you and I'll get it done," she cried.

Pamela slowly stood up from the sofa and walked over to Face and Tasha. "Face, don't worry. Me and Tasha will both be here for you. If you need us for anything, just call us on the phone at the main office. But, right now, you need to get out of this house as soon as possible," she said.

"She's right, Baby. They're probably searching for you right now, so they can keep a close eye on you."

Face walked over and sat down on the sofa. Pamela and Tasha stood there watching as he sat back in deep thought. Suddenly, he snapped out of his concentrated state and said, "I have a feeling that they're out there watching me right now. And I have a plan to find out."

Face reached for the telephone and quickly dialed a number. A man's voice answered and Face sat back and explained what he wanted him to do. After he hung up the phone, he looked up at both women and said, "Go grab y'all's purses and keys. We're all going to the movies!"

"The movies?" Tasha questioned.

"Yeah, the movies. I'll explain everything to y'all in the car. Now, let's hurry," he said, standing up from the sofa.

Fifteen minutes later Face, Tasha and Pamela all left the condominium and walked into the dark, windless night.

After they all got into Tasha's brand new champagne colored S-600 Mercedes Benz, Tasha slowly pulled off and headed towards Delaware Avenue's movie complex, and just as Face had suspected, the Feds were watching.

Tasha calmly drove, as a tinted, dark colored Ford Taurus closely trailed her car. Every turn she made, it did the same. As Tasha continued to drive, Face was on one of his cell phone talking to one of his top men, "Shut down everything, immediately! The milk is spoiled!"

'The milk is spoiled' was the code message that meant the emergency shutdown of the whole operation.

After Face made a few more calls, Face closed his phone, got comfortable in his seat and closed his eyes.

CHAPTER 86

Twenty minutes later…

Tasha drove her Mercedes into the movie theatre parking lot and found an empty space. Together they all walked toward the entrance. The tinted Ford Taurus that was parked a few spaces away with the two FBI agents that were inside watched their every move. As soon as they paid and entered the theatre, Face hurried and rushed towards the men's bathroom. When he walked inside Quincy was standing there holding a shopping bag. They were

both dressed alike; blue jeans, grey sweatshirt, white Nike running shoes and blue fitted baseball cap.

"The milk has been spoiled," Face said, quickly changing into the white sweat suit that Quincy had brought him. "In the mean time, I want you to do a few things for me," Face said,

reaching into his pocket and taking out a small piece of paper. He passed the paper to Quincy and watched as he read it.

"Don't worry, I'll take care of everything," Quincy replied.

They shook hands and both walked out of the bathroom.

After Face had given Tasha and Pamela a kiss and a hug, they watched as he walked over to the side exit door and calmly stepped outside. Face walked through the crowded parking lot and stopped when he approached a parked tinted, black Dodge Magnum. With the key that Quincy had gave him, he quickly got inside. Moments later he was driving by the parked Ford Taurus, straight out of the parking lot exit. He was headed to his highly secured, secret safe house in East Hampton, New York where he could lay low and figure things out.

When Tasha and Pamela had walked out of the theatre Quincy was with them. They all got into Tasha's Mercedes and moments later she pulled off. Once again the tinted Ford Taurus closely trailed them.

Agent McDonald closed his cell phone and looked at his partner, Agent Powaski and said, "After tomorrow, Face's reign on top will be all over!"

As he continued to follow Tasha's car, Powaski just smiled and nodded his head. "Did they get the Gomez brothers?" he asked.

"Yeah, in New York. About an hour ago," McDonald replied. "And they also got Face on a recorded phone conversation with Roberto Chavez discussing the purchase of over 2000 kilos

of cocaine and 250 pounds of heroin. Now, all we need to do is catch Face dropping off the money and picking up the drugs!"

"So, Roberto had decided to flip sides, huh?" Powaski asked as he drove.

"Yeah, he's being placed in the witness protection program as we speak. He's already agreed to testify against Face and the Gomez brothers. With Roberto's cooperation all three of

them will soon be serving life sentences," McDonald said grinning.

"Maybe we need to talk to a few of Face's friends who are in prison; give them a chance to get some of that hard time off their backs. It would make our case stronger at trial," Agent Powaski said.

"That's not a bad idea. In the next few weeks we'll go pay some of them a visit. There's not a prisoner alive that don't want his freedom," McDonald said and they both started laughing.

"Do you want to keep trailing them?" Powaski asked, as he followed Tasha's car down Market Street.

"No, turn off at the next corner. We've seen enough for one day."

At the corner of 17th and Market street the Ford Taurus made a quick right turn. On their way back to the FBI office, the two agents had no idea that Face was cruising down the New Jersey Turnpike, already half way to New York City.

Northeast Philly, early the next morning, 8:17 AM...

Quincy was watching the house, a block away, from inside a tinted Infiniti G-35. For the past hour he had set and closely watched everything through the lens of the black binoculars

in his hands. The Feds had no idea that they too were being watched by one of Face's top men, who in turn, was reporting everything directly back to him.

Quincy watched as the Feds cleared the area. They had armed undercover agents posted on the tops of buildings and inside unmarked cars. After seeing Roberto Chavez being driven by two undercover agents, Quincy started up his car, made a u-turn, and drove in the opposite direction.

"Face, I just saw him pull up. It's true man, he's trying to set you up with the Feds. The whole thing is one big set up!" Quincy said into his cell phone.

"Good job, Quincy. And thanks for taking care of everything else. I'll be talking to you soon," Face said ending the phone call.

Face sat up on the edge of the bed and dialed the Gomez's private line. Once again there was no answer. After closing up his phone, he decided not to call them again-not until they

tried to contact him. Face wasn't sure what was going on, but the one thing that he did know was that he had to try and remain as calm as possible. He had been laying in bed all night thinking. He knew the Feds didn't have much on him; only the things Roberto had to tell them. And most of it was probably lies, designed to save his own ass. Still, Face knew exactly how the Feds played; by their own crooked rules. Face also knew how badly they wanted to take him down and use him as an example. Being young, rich and black only made him a bigger and better target for them.

A few hours later...

Inside the U.S. Federal Courthouse in downtown Philadelphia, a secret Grand Jury convened and was in progress. Inside the Grand Jury Room, the Assistant United States Attorney was presenting his case against Face to the jury. Also present were Agents Powaski and McDonald, Philadelphia Police Detective Ron Perry, a government assistant for Senator C.W. Watson and the governments number one witness, Roberto Chavez.

When Face didn't show up at the FBI and DEA secret undercover drug sting operation, they decided to try for an indictment anyway. Even with the minimum amount of evidence they had, they believed it was enough to convince the Jury that Face needed to be taken off the streets.

Less than one hour after the jury had been impaneled they had come to a unanimous decision. With the evidence and the testimony from the government's witnesses they had voted to

issue a federal indictment.

"We got him!" Ron Perry said, as he and the two agents walked out of the courtroom.

"That's right, Detective. Once the bench warrant is issued, which should be later today, all we have to do then is find Face and arrest him," Agent Powaski said. Maybe he'll do us all a favor and resist arrest!" he added, then they all started laughing.

CHAPTER 87

Two weeks later...

For two long weeks Face hid inside his luxurious New York estate. The only people who knew his whereabouts were Tasha, Pamela, Quincy and his good friend and financial advisor, Peter J. Greenberg. They were the only people he trusted. Most days Face sat around watching CNN and reading newspapers. Afterwards he would go for a workout in his state of the art gym, then take a hot relaxing shower. At night he would eat while lying in bed thinking, then call Tasha and the kids and talk with them before he went to sleep.

He knew that the main keys to his success were to learn as much about his case as possible, and to stay calm. To panic would spell doom and ruin. Not just for him but for his family as well. As he sat on the sofa watching CNN, the front door opened and Tasha walked inside. She smiled, ran over to Face and joined him on the sofa. Without words they started intensely kissing and hugging.

Almost every day after work, Tasha would get in her Mercedes and drive to New York to see him. After their long passionate kiss, Face looked deep into her watery eyes and asked, "did you make sure nobody was trying to follow you again?"

"Yes, Baby. I took the directions you gave me and made sure nobody was trailing me," she said, as the tears started to roll down her face.

Face reached out and grabbed Tasha into his arms. She laid her head on his chest and said, " FBI agents came by the job and house again looking for you. I told them that I still haven't seen or heard from you in weeks."

"Anything else?" Face asked.

"Your mother misses you terribly. And Veronica said, if there's anything she could do for you, just let her know and it's done. I also gave the rest of the money that Quincy dropped off to Peter. He already took care of everything," Tasha said, as she looked up and smiled. "Norman and Isuri miss their daddy," she added.

"Did you tell them that I would be gone for a while?"

"Yes, I told them. But, they still miss you," she replied.

"Did the Gomez brothers get in contact with you, yet?" she asked.

"No, I haven't heard from them since that night they called me and told me about Roberto. I'm thinking they're out of the country somewhere," Face stated.

"Do you think Roberto told on them also?" Tasha asked curiously.

After a short sigh Face said, "I've thought about it a few times and I still don't know what to think. If Roberto tried to set me up with the Feds, then maybe he did the same with the Gomez brothers too. If he did then he knows the consequences for his betrayal. Still, right now, only time will tell."

Tasha sat up and said, "So, why haven't you gotten a lawyer yet? Your old lawyer, James Blake, called me a few times asking about you. He wants to help."

"That's what I wanted to talk to you about," Face said, as he reached into his shirt pocket and took out a small piece of paper. "I want you to get me this lawyer. Her name is Gloria Jones and she's the only person that I want to represent me," he said passing Tasha the paper.

Tasha looked at Gloria Jones's name and just nodded her head. She knew exactly who she was. Tasha had never forgotten about the farewell letter that she wrote to Face those many years ago. She also knew that Gloria Jones was a woman who deeply loved Face and decided to leave town because she couldn't have him.

"Is this all, cause I'll get right on it," Tasha asked.

Face reached over and grabbed Tasha's hands and looked into her eyes. "No, that's not all. There's something about me and Gloria Jones that you need to know," he said.

Tasha sat back and listened while Face told her all about his past relationship with Gloria Jones. After he finished Tasha was relieved to finally know the whole truth.

"I'll go and see her tomorrow morning and let her know everything," Tasha said, as she and Face stood up from the sofa.

As they walked over toward the stairs one of the maids approached them, "Mr. and Mrs. Smith would y'all like any special orders for tonight?" she politely asked.

"No Anna, we'll be fine. Just make sure that me and my wife are not disturbed tonight," Face said, as he grabbed Tasha's hand. With huge smiles, they headed to the cozy master suite upstairs.

S.C.I. Graterford Prison...

Agents McDonald and Powaski sat inside the small staff room patiently waiting for the prison staff to bring in the next inmate. The two agents had taken the trip from Philly to hopefully gather more witnesses and vital information for their case against Face.

The door opened and the two C.O.s escorted the next inmate inside. Standing there with a newly full grown beard and a few pounds heavier was Face's right hand man, Reese. His wrists were handcuffed and shackled tightly to a waist chain. After Reese sat down in a chair the two C.O.s left the room and closed the door.

"How are you Mr. Daniels. My name is Agent McDonald and this is my partner Agent Powaski. We're with the FBI..."

Reese gave the agents an angry disgusted look and said, "What the fuck do y'all want!"

Agent McDonald grinned and said, "Reese, we are here to help you. And maybe give you a chance."

"A chance for what?" Reese replied with a curious look.

"A chance at saving yourself from a future life sentence. And a chance to be back with your new wife, Sandy and your pretty little daughter, Amiaya," Powaski said.

Reese sat back and smiled, "Is that right?" he said nonchalantly, "Look here, y'all wasted y'all's time coming up here."

"No, you look here, Mr. Daniels! Your friend Face is in a lot of trouble. Too much for even him to get out of. I know by now that you know about everything that's going on. And your name has been brought up quite a few times. Now, either you can work with us and we'll go to the U.S. Attorney with a recommendation that you and your family be placed in the Witness Protection Program, or you can join your friend. Reese, this case is bigger than anything you could ever imagine and your friend, Face, is going down with or without you," Agent McDonald

threatened.

"If you do decide to be loyal to your friend, then we will have to come after you as well. And based on all the witnesses and evidence we now have, we will pursue a life sentence. That's natural life! Not like here in the state prison. Federal life means until you die," Agent Powaski added with a sly grin.

"We know everything, Reese. So try and save yourself. Or at least do it for your family," McDonald said, as he stood up and walked over to the door.

"Think about this, Reese. Would Face do a life sentence for you if the shoe was on the other foot? Would he choose you over his family?" Powaski asked.

With a calm expression, Reese sat there in total silence. Then, moments later, the two C.O.s escorted him out of the room.

"So, what do you think?" Powaski asked as they walked down the hall.

"We just have to cross our fingers and wait and see," McDonald answered.

CHAPTER 88

Manhattan, New York, early the next morning...

In the heart of New York City, Tasha got out the Yellow Cab and walked into a tall office building. After walking through the crowded lobby, she and a few other people rushed to an awaiting elevator. When the elevator doors closed, she pushed the button for the 12th floor and stood back. Holding a black briefcase in her hands, Tasha was dressed to impress. With her hair and nails freshly done, she was wearing a cream colored business suit with a matching pair of Gucci sandals.

Four men were on the elevator with her and none of them could keep their eyes off of her. As she stood there waiting for the elevator to reach her floor she could feel their eyes scanning her entire body. She was used to the attention that men, and sometimes women, would give her. But Tasha never paid it any mind. Her mind, body and soul, yearned for one man only. Her husband, Face.

When the elevator stopped on the 12th floor and the large steel doors slowly opened, Tasha stepped out and into the small lobby. She walked over to a young attractive white woman sitting behind a desk and typing on a computer.

"Excuse me, my name is Tasha Smith. I'm here to meet with Mrs. Gloria Jones-Henderson."

"One moment, please," the woman said, picking up the phone, pushing a number, then waiting.

"Yes, Lori, what is it?" Gloria answered.

"Mrs. Henderson, Mrs. Tasha Smith is here to see you," she said, smiling at Tasha.

"Okay, send her back," Gloria said, then hung up the phone.

"You can go right back. Mrs. Henderson's office is down that hall, the second door on the right," Lori pointed out.

"Thank you," Tasha smiled, then turned and walked down the hallway. She felt envious eyes on her back.

When she reached the door she read the sign on it, 'Gloria Jones-Henderson, Attorney at Law'. She knocked twice and when the door opened Gloria was standing there with a big smile on her face.

"Glad to meet you Mrs. Smith," Gloria said, taking Tasha's hand. After their handshake, Gloria led Tasha into her large plush office and offered her a comfortable seat in front of her desk. Tasha sat down and Gloria walked around her desk and sat down in her high-backed, black leather chair. "Wow, I've been a big fan of yours since reading your story in Ebony a few years ago. It's truly an honor to meet you," Gloria said with excitement.

"Thank you. I'm a big fan of yours, also," Tasha said. "I read a story on you in Essence a few months back. And I must say, you are a lot prettier in person," she added.

"Thank you," Gloria blushed. "Now, tell me what was so important that you needed to see me as soon as possible?"

Tasha looked deep into Gloria's eyes and said, "You don't remember me, do you?" "Excuse me? Am I missing something?" Gloria asked with a puzzled look. She stared for a moment in silence, then it dawned on her. "You're...You're Tasha! I recognize you now! It's been a while, but I remember you!"

"Well, I'm his wife now, and that's why I came all the way to New York City to see you," Tasha said with a ruthless look.

"You and Face are married?"

"Yes, Mrs. Henderson and we have two young children now," Tasha replied. Gloria sank back into her comfortable, soft leather chair and smiled. "Did Face ever tell you about..."

"Y'all's brief affair," Tasha interrupted. "Yes, he told me everything."

Concerned, Gloria asked, "How is he doing?"

"Not too good. That's why I'm here."

"What's wrong?" Gloria asked.

After a long sigh, Tasha tearfully looked at Gloria and said, "my husband was recently indicted by a Federal Grand Jury in Philadelphia. The Feds have a bench warrant out for his arrest and a one-hundred thousand dollar reward," Tasha explained between her sobs.

"For what?!" Gloria asked in surprise.

"For drugs! My husband was set up by a man named Roberto Chevez, a Nicaraguan citizen who was here in the U.S. on a temporary work visa. Mr. Chevez got my husband to incriminate himself on a recorded phone conversation that was being recorded by the FBI,"

Tasha explained.

Gloria sat back with her arms crossed carefully listening to everything that Tasha told her. Mrs. Henderson have you ever heard the name, C.W. Watson?"

"Yes, he's a U.S. Senator, and a good friend of my husband's. But, what has he got to do with this?"

"My husband believes that he is one of the men that C.W. Watson has been after since becoming head of the Domestic Anti-Drug Commission," Tasha said.

Gloria grabbed a pen and a yellow legal pad and began to scribble notes. "Does Face know you're here?"

"He's the one who sent me to come and see you. He's been keeping a close eye on you. He knows all about your reputation as one of the best, young defense attorneys in the country."

Gloria smiled at the compliments. "So, tell me, Mrs. Smith, how can I help?"

"Face wants you and only you to represent him. We'll pay whatever the cost," Tasha said, with a sincere expression. "Money is not an obstacle," she added.

"Where is your husband now?" Gloria asked.

"He's at our house in the Hamptons. He's been there for the past few weeks."

"Face is in New York?" Gloria asked, surprised.

"Yes, Mrs. Henderson. Face has been hiding from the authorities, trying to put his thoughts in order. He's safe at the house. No one knows about it except a few close friends, and now you. So, will you represent my husband, Mrs. Henderson?... Right now, Face really needs you. He told me to tell you that," Tasha stated.

Gloria looked at Tasha and smiled. Then she said, "Please, call me Gloria. And yes, it would be an honor to help out a good friend."

Tasha sat her briefcase on her lap and opened it up, then she reached inside and took out a piece of paper with an address and a phone number written on it. "Here, this is for you, Gloria.

It's the address and phone number to the house. Face is already expecting your call or visit," Tasha said with a smile that reached her eyes.

"So, he knew that I wouldn't say no, huh?" Gloria asked, as she took the paper from her hand.

"My husband said that y'all were good friends, and that real friends always come through."

Gloria watched as Tasha reached into the briefcase again and brought out her check book. She closed the briefcase and lay the check book on top of it and began to write. When she finished Tasha passed the check to Gloria. Gloria stared at the check with a stunned expression.

"Mrs. Smith,..." Gloria started.

"Please call me Tasha," Tasha interrupted with a smile.

"Tasha, this is way more than enough!"

"It's all yours, Gloria. My husband wanted to cover all expenses; traveling costs, hotels, phone calls, taxis and whatever else you need to do your job comfortably. Face is planning on taking this case to trial and he's prepared to go down fighting!"

Gloria sat back holding the check in her hands. "If everything you told me today is true then it's going to be a long drawn out trial. The United States Government has all the resources

to fight these type of drug cases. And as we both know, the U.S. Government does not like to lose!"

Tasha closed her briefcase and stood up, "and neither does my husband," she said acutely.

After Gloria walked her to the door, they shook hands again and Tasha stepped out of the office and gently closed the door behind her. As soon as the door had closed, Gloria walked back to her desk and sat down. She picked the check up again and looked at it closely, as if to make sure her eyes weren't deceiving her. They weren't, so she reached for the phone and made the first of many important phone calls.

CHAPTER 89

Lewisburg Federal Prison...

Vernon 'Truck' Wilson stepped inside the small interview room. He was being escorted by a large white, angry looking and bitter C.O. that treated the shackled and handcuffed prisoner none to gently. "Sit down!" the C.O. sneered, impatiently urging Truck into the chair.

"You can leave us now," Agent McDonald told the C.O. in a superior tone.

The C.O. grinned patronizingly then turned and went out the door. He glared at Truck as he left.

"Who the fuck is he?" Powaski asked as the door closed.

"That's Stripe, 'The Stripe' for the yellow streak down his back. Unless he got a prisoner chained down. Then he a bad muthafucker," Truck smiled, as he looked at the two Agents inconspicuously. What's this all about?"

"Your freedom, if you're willing to play by the rules," McDonald replied.

Truck sat back and started laughing. "I think y'all got the wrong man!" he laughed.

Agent Powaski scooted his chair closer to Truck and stared directly in his eyes. "Mr. Wilson you have been in prison for over eight years and you have a long way to go before you're eligible for release. You know why we are here and either you're gonna help us out or not!"

"I ain't no snitch!" Truck replied.

He watched as McDonald reached into a large brown envelope and pulled out a white sheet of paper.

"Do you see this piece of paper, Mr. Wilson? Here, why don't you read it for yourself," he said, handing it to Truck.

Truck sat back in the chair and carefully read every line. When he had finished reading the paper he laid it aside and looked at the two agents. "This says that if I'm willing to cooperate and testify against Norman Smith, Junior, aka Black Scarface, then the U.S. Government will recommend that the rest of my sentence be vacated and I'll be placed in the Witness Protection Program," Truck said with an incredulous expression.

"That's right, Mr. Wilson and it's signed by the Director of the FBI himself. All we'll need from you is for you to take the witness stand and tell the jury what we need for you to say. We already have a list made out for you," Agent McDonald said with a sly smile.

"So, basically what the government wants is for me to lie on the witness stand. Commit perjury for my freedom?"

"Call it what you like. But, think about your freedom," Powaski replied.

"Y'all want Face that bad?" Truck asked.

"More than you could ever imagine, Mr. Wilson, and with or without your help, Face is going down. Mark my words," McDonald said.

Washington, D.C...

C.W. Watson sat behind his large ornate, antique desk looking over some very highly classified documents. Since being appointed head of the Domestic Anti-Drug Commission, every man on his list of major drug dealers, except one, had been arrested and charged. The one remaining name was Norman 'Face' Smith, Jr.. The Senator was going over material for his press conference that was less than an hour away.

Expected to be in attendance were members from all the major news media; NBC, CBS, ABC, CNN, NPR, and the BBC. All were expected to carry live coverage on their radio and TV stations nationwide.

C.W. Watson was ready to let the national public know just who he was and at the same time diminish the character of the only fugitive that had yet to be caught and arrested from his

list. For C.W. Watson it was all a powerful political move; fooling the public with the 'good guys versus the bad guys' scheme that the U.S. Government was a master at using.

After closing the classified document folder, the Senator stood from his desk and stretched his arms out and mumbled, "I'm sorry Mr. Smith, but you're the perfect 'fall-guy' that

I need to win my place in the White House's Oval Office! It's my destiny!"

C.W. grabbed his briefcase and headed for the door. He had people to impress!

Philadelphia, PA. early the next morning...

A swarm of Federal agents from the FBI, DEA, ATF, local police and Philadelphia County Sheriff's Department raided more than thirty-five locations suspected of being connected to Face's drug operation. Unbeknownst to the authorities, Face's entire drug operation had already been shut down for weeks, and none of his top men had been arrested. The 'spoiled milk' alert proved that Face had remained three steps ahead of the authorities.

For all the federal authorities involved in the morning raids, it turned out to be one big disappointment and another big waste of tax-payer's money.

Still, after yesterday's live televised press conference, Norman 'Face' Smith, Jr. was now the 'Most Wanted Man in America!' And C.W. Watson had made himself into the new public hero that was determined to take down the bad guy.

Inside the T&F Real Estate Firm...

Pamela stepped into Tasha's office and quickly closed the door. "A group of reporters are all outside in the lobby. What do you want to do?" Pamela asked, taking a seat.

Tasha put down the newspaper she had been reading and said, "Nothing. Face said don't do anything. I already called a two o'clock meeting to inform all of our employees to avoid the media and don't answer any questions about anything. If anyone talks to the media they will be fired on the spot!"

"I see you've been reading the news papers. Those bastards are trying to ruin my son!" Pamela vented.

Tasha picked up the newspaper and showed Pamela the bold black headlines, 'PHILLY DRUG KINGPIN ON THE RUN FROM THE FEDS'

"'Trying' is an understatement!" Tasha replied angrily.

"They're making Face out to be some kind of violent street thug! Feeding the public with a bunch of bullshit!" Pamela vented, as her eyes filled with tears.

Tasha tearfully looked at Pamela and said, "Don't worry, Miss Pam. We're gonna fight these people with everything we got!"

East Hampton, Long Island, New York...

Gloria sat beside Face staring into his deep brown eyes. To her, he was still the most handsome and intelligent man she had ever known. And deep down inside, her feelings for him

had never changed.

"I made a few very important calls and Face, this thing don't look good at all," she told him. "The press conference that C.W. Watson did yesterday started a media frenzy. Now, the public thinks you're some type of mastermind, murderously bloody, drug dealer."

"But, I wasn't indicted for no murders," Face said.

"We know that, but the public don't and the media will use any information, valid or not, to create a story. It sells papers," Gloria replied.

Face sat back nodding his head. "So, honestly, what do you think, Gloria?"

After a long sigh, Gloria reached out and grabbed both of Face's hands. "They want you bad Face. More than John Gotti, Ricky Ross and Larry Hoover all combined. This thing is big

and I believe there are a lot of powerful people involved, pulling strings to make sure you go down!"

"Can you beat 'em?"

Tears welled up in Gloria's eyes and started falling down her cheeks. "I can try," she said softly.

Face reached over and gave Gloria a long warm hug. "Just do your best," he whispered in her ear.

"I will. I promise you!" she replied, looking into his eyes and said, "Tomorrow morning we're driving to Philadelphia so you can turn yourself in. The longer you run, the worse it gets."

Face nodded his head in agreement and said, "I'll be ready."

Then he and Gloria stood up from the sofa and he walked her over to the door. After she left the house, Face retreated back into his bedroom. He laid on his bed and stared at the twelve foot ceiling.

CHAPTER 90

Philadelphia, early the next morning...

Face and his lawyer, Gloria Jones, walked into the downtown FBI office to turn himself in to the authorities. After being read his rights, he was fingerprinted, photographed and then processed into the federal system. His new federal prison number was 84546-066.

After Face was processed he was quickly escorted to the nearby Federal Detention Center. Face was housed on the 4th floor with other federal inmates waiting to be sentenced or waiting to go to trial.

Early the next morning, four U.S. Marshals escorted Face to his arraignment hearing inside the federal court building. At Face arraignment, he and Gloria stood side by side while

a magistrate judge read Face the charges against him. Face was being charged with conspiracy to purchase and distribute more than 2000 kilograms of Cocaine and 250 kilos of Heroin. If found guilty he would be sentenced to life in federal prison without the possibility of parole.

The day after his arraignment, he was denied bond because he was considered to be a major flight risk, even though he had voluntarily surrendered. However, the government didn't want to take any chances.

The case was assigned to Federal District Judge, Anthony T. Marino, a conservative, mild-tempered man that had been a Federal District Judge for 23 years. Judge Marino was respected by all his peers and considered a fair judge. The Assistant United States Attorney assigned to represent the government's case was Vincent L. Brady, a tall, slim, white man with a hard nose reputation and a flawless record. In his 12 years, as a U.S. Prosecutor for the Eastern District of Pennsylvania, he had never lost a case. His reputation was the reason the government had specially appointed him to

Face's case. They wanted Face badly, and Vincent L. Brady was the man to take him down.

A few days later...

Inside his cell at the federal detention center Face was laying across his bunk reading a few important documents that Gloria sent him. When a C.O. opened his door, he quickly sat up on his bunk.

"Smith, this is your new celly," the C.O. said, shoving a tall, slim, dark skinned man into the cell and slamming the steel door.

Face stared at the man and thought that he looked familiar. He was positive that he knew the man from somewhere, but he just couldn't place him.

"Hey, what's up? I'm Kevon," the man said, extending his hand.

"Face," Face replied, as he shook the man's hand.

"Wow, it's kinda cool that I'm in the same cell with one of the biggest drug dealers in the whole country," Kevon said with a smile.

Face didn't reply, he just curiously watched as Kevon made up his bunk. "Don't I know you from somewhere?" Face asked curiously.

"I doubt it. I'm just a petty drug dealer from North Philly, "Kevon answered.

"Where at in North?"

"Richard Allen Projects," Kevon answered proudly.

Face made a mental note of that and then laid back across his bunk.

"Man, you all over the TV and newspapers! Everybody is talking about you!"

"Yeah, I know," Face said, as he finished reading his documents.

After Kevon finished making up his bunk, he climbed up on top of it and laid down. "So you think you can win?" Kevon asked as he leaned over and looked down from his bunk.

Face looked up at Kevon's familiar face and said, "Only time will tell. One thing for sure… I'm gonna fight with every breath I got.

Kevon smiled and nodded his head. "I wish you luck," he said, as he laid back down.

After two weeks inside the Federal Detention Center...

Face had spent the majority of his time reading over important documents about his case. The only time he left his cell was for mail call or for a visit. And to all the other inmates there,

Face was looked upon as a celebrity. Even members of the staff were in awe of him. They couldn't believe that the man who was considered the biggest drug dealer in the country was right there with them.

As for his celly, Kevon, Face still couldn't place his face or figure out where he knew him from. For the two weeks that they had been cellies, Face had people secretly gathering up enough

information to find out who he really was. Face didn't trust anyone around him. Especially a talkative cellmate who asked too many questions and never stopped running his mouth.

Inside the private Attorney's visiting room, Face and Gloria sat there talking and discussing some strategies for the trial.

"This is your Motion For Discovery," Gloria said, passing Face a manila folder. "Now you can see for yourself all the government's witnesses that's gonna testify against you at the trial. You'll also see the statements they made and swore to."

Face opened the folder and looked over his Motion For Discovery. As he perused each page he couldn't believe what he was reading. After a long sigh he looked up at Gloria and shook his head in total disappointment and disbelief. "Damn!" he mumbled under his breath.

"As you see Face, there are no friends in this ugly game. Even the ones you think are your friends will cross you to save their own asses," Gloria stated. "The government is the very best at turning your friends and loved ones against you," she added.

"I still can't believe it!" Face replied.

"Well, believe it! Every name on those pages are people who have made deals with the government to take you down. Most likely after they testify against you at trial they'll each enter into the Witness Protection Program."

Face closed the folder and passed it back to Gloria. His mind was clouded with thoughts, and his soul was filled with indescribable pain. He still couldn't believe that people who he considered friends were all going to testify against him.

"Face!" Gloria said, snapping him from out of his daze.

"Yeah ?"

"I checked up on your celly like you asked," she said.

"What did you find out?"

"I don't know what's going on, but there's no inmate Kevon Johnson, prisoner number 73852-066 anywhere in the system. I can't find anything on the guy. Make sure you watch him very closely. He might be an informant working with the Feds to try and gather information on you. So, be extra careful."

"Did you talk to Quincy?"

"Yeah, I spoke with Quincy yesterday and he told me to tell you that no one down at the Richard Allen

Projects has ever heard of the guy. So, please, be cautious and watch what you say," Gloria warned.

"Don't worry, I'll take care of it," Face grinned.

Gloria closed her briefcase and stood up. Then Face stood up and gave her a hug.

"Thanks Gloria, for everything. I really appreciate it." Gloria stared into his handsome face and smiled. Just being in his presence turned her on more than any man she had ever known, including her husband. "You don't have to thank me, Face. That's what friends are for," she said softly.

After Face was escorted back to his cell, Gloria walked out of the visiting room and headed straight down the hall. Before she left the building tears of pain, sadness, confusion and love were all falling from the confines of her eyes.

CHAPTER 91

When Face had returned back to his cell, Kevon was sitting in a chair reading one of Face's newspapers. Face quickly closed the door and rushed right toward him. After knocking Kevon to the floor, Face pinned him down and placed both hands around his throat. Kevon tried his best to fight him off, but Face was too strong, and his tight grip was slowly taking his breath away.

"Motherfucker, I don't know who you are or why you're here. But, if you don't pack your shit up and get the fuck out of this cell, you'll be dead before dinner time!" Face said with a grave look.

Face watched as Kevon gagged for air. His eyes were wide with fear and his face was as red as an apple. "Do you hear me, muthafucker!?" Face yelled out. "Do you!?"

Kevon nodded his head and Face got off him. With a look of total fear, he struggled to his feet and rushed out of the cell. A few moments later, two C.O.s came to Face's cell and packed up all of Kevon's personal belongings. They did it without saying a single word to him. Before leaving the cell one of the C.O.s turned to him and said, "Mr. Smith, for the rest of your time here, at FDC, you won't get any more cellmates."

Face watched as the C.O.s left the cell and shut the door behind him. After they were gone Face laid on his bunk and finished thinking about all of his former friends who had turned against him.

* * *

Inside a small staff room on the first floor of the detention center Agent Powaski sat across from his visibly shaken partner. "You all right, Jeff?" he asked, as he passed McDonald a cold glass of water.

"Yeah, I'll be fine," he said. "That son of a bitch almost killed me."

"We can say he knew who you were and charge him with assault," Powaski told him.

"No, that won't be necessary, and besides, we don't need the media to get a hold of this," Agent McDonald said, rubbing around his throat.

Agent Powaski slammed his fist down on the table and said, "We should get his ass for what he did to you!"

"Don't worry partner, Face is going down and we'll both get the last laugh. I plan on sending him a card once in a while, while he serving out his life sentence," Agent McDonald

said, as they both started laughing.

"So, do you think he ever figured out who you are?"

"No, he ain't gotta clue that I was Bam-Bam, the same man that took down his friend Truck. I just wish I could have gotten some vital information out of him, but the kid don't talk much," Agent McDonald said, before taking another sip of water.

"So, do you think the two weeks you spent as his celly, was a waste of time?"

"I think so. Face rarely talked about his case. Most times he just sat there reading stuff his lawyer sent to him. Did you get anything from his phone conversations?"

"Nothing! All we were able to get was some meaningless conversations with his mother, wife and children. I'm sure he watched what he said on the phone," Powaski replied. Roberto said he was a very smart young man," McDonald said.

"What do you think of his lawyer?"

"She's a very beautiful young woman but way over her head, and I think she knows it," McDonald replied with a grin. "Vincent Bradley is gonna eat her ass alive!" he added.

Both men stood up and walked out of the room. As they walked down the hallway McDonald asked, "Are all the witnesses ready?"

"As ready as they will ever be," Powaski replied.

One week later...

Inside his Washington, D.C. office, Senator C.W. Watson and U.S. Prosecutor Vincent L. Bradley were talking about the upcoming trial.

"So, is everything set in motion?" C.W. said, as he closed up the white folder he had just finished reading.

"Yes, Mr. Watson, everything is set and the witnesses have already made their statements and are ready to testify at trial," Vincent said grinningly.

"Good. Very, very good, I want to make an example out of this low-life thug!" C.W. said.

"And we will. With all the evidence and witnesses we have against Mr. Smith, there's nothing in this world that could save him from a life sentence! Nothing!"

"I'm proud of you, Vincent. And like I promised you, if you win this case and get this man off the streets, I'll going to bring you here to work with me in D.C." C.W. replied. "I need strong hard working men like yourself," he added.

"Thank you Mr. Watson, it would be an honor. And don't you worry, Mr. Smith is as good as gone. We got his prison cell already waiting," Vincent said as both men laughed.

* * *

Pamela and Veronica sat across from Face inside the crowded visiting room at the Federal Detention Center. A few C.O.s were situated throughout the room keeping a close eye on both the visitors and inmates.

"Your Judge is Anthony T. Marino?" Veronica asked excitedly.

"Yeah, that's who was assigned to rule over my case," Face answered. "Why, do you know him?"

"Yes, I know Anthony very well," Veronica said, with a smile.

"Maybe you can go have a talk with him," Pamela said. Anything right now will help," she added.

"Don't worry, I'll take care of it. As a matter of fact, I'm supposed to see him later this evening," Veronica said. "He's due for his weekly appointment," she grinned.

"Hell no! Tell me you're joking!" Pamela said with excitement.

"Believe me, I would not be joking at a time like this. Anthony has been a very good friend of mine for quite some time."

"Well, just see what you can do for me. I will really appreciate it," Face said in all seriousness. "They're trying to hang me!"

Veronica reached over and placed her soft manicured hands on Face's hand and said, "Don't worry Face, I'ma do everything in my power to help you out"

"Thank you, Veronica," Face said as he reached out and gave her a hug. "That guy, C.W. Watson is really trying his best to destroy me!"

Veronica looked up perplexed. "Did you say C.W. Watson? she asked.

"Yeah, he's a United St..."

"States Senator," Veronica said, finishing Face's sentence.

"You know him, too?" Pamela asked with a smile.

"No, but I do know somebody who does," she grinned.

"Who?" Pamela asked curiously.

Veronica looked at Pamela and just shook her head in total disbelief.

"Who, girl?" Pamela repeated.

"I know his Godson," Veronica finally said.

"Who the hell is his Godson?" Face asked.

After a long sigh, Veronica said, "Senator C.W. Watson is the Godfather to Charles Klein, the Mayor of Philadelphia, and one of my most loyal clients. Small world, huh?"

Pamela and Face both sat there with doubtful looks.

"Do...Do...Do you got the Mayor on tape?" Face asked.

A devilish smile came to Veronica's face as she said, "Yeah, I have Charles and Anthony on tape. Along with many other powerful and influential people in this city."

"Oh, my God!" Pamela said, as tears started to fall down her face.

"That ain't all," Veronica said. Her sly grin showing that there was so much more she hadn't yet revealed.

"What else?" Face asked.

"I got the Mayor drunk on tape, talking about an incident he was involved in with his father, Tom and C.W. Watson. I've watched it a few times and it still freaks me out," Veronica

replied.

"What is it?" Face asked her.

Veronica moved her chair closer and they all gathered around in a small huddle.

In a low whispering voice she said, "It happened a long time ago in West Virginia..."

Downtown Philadelphia...

Inside Peter J. Greenberg's plush office, Tasha sat across from his desk reading over her husband's offshore account records. After she perused the documents, Tasha passed the file back to Peter with a pleased look. "Good job Peter. I'm visiting with my husband in a few hours. I'll let him know that everything is in order."

"Tasha, your husband is not only my top client. But, he is also a very good friend of mine. And like I told both of you guys, I'll make sure every single penny he has is safe and secured."

"Have the Feds been here asking you any questions?" Tasha asked.

"Yes, they came by here about a month ago", he replied.

"What happened?"

"Nothing really happened. They were just asking me a lot of questions about me and Face's relationship," Peter grinned.

"And what did you say to them?"

"I told them that you're my client and I only know your husband through working with you. I'm sure they believe that there's a lot more to it, but there's nothing they could do

about it. Face was five steps ahead of them," Peter said with a laugh. "Tasha, your husband is one of the smartest men I've ever known. Even I learned a lot from working with him!" he said

honestly.

"Thank you, Peter. I'll be sure to tell him what you said when I go visit him," Tasha said, as she grabbed her briefcase and stood up from the chair.

After shaking hands, Peter watched as Tasha walked towards the door. "Tasha?"

She paused and turned around, "Yes, Peter?"

"Make sure you tell Face that if he needs me for anything at all, I'm here for him."

"I will."

"And that I'm really sorry about his friends turning on him. Who would ever believe it, huh?"

Tasha looked at Peter and sighed, then she said, "The Bible says that a friend loves at all times. So, everyone that's testifying against my husband were not his friends in the first place."

Then Peter watched as Tasha turned and walked out of his office.

* * *

Parked right down the street from the Federal Building, located on 6th and Arch street, Quincy sat inside his tinted Dodge Magnum and watched as one of Face's former top street lieutenants walked into the building. The man's name was Gary 'Knuckles' Robertson, and Quincy learned that he was secretly talking to the Feds.

Quincy had also learned that Knuckles had a deep personal hatred for Reese, for taking his girl, Passion, from him many years ago. To make matters worse, Reese had also beaten him up outside her job and pistol whipped him in front of people who had respected and feared him. For that reason and so many others, that no one knew about, Knuckles was working with the FBI as a paid informant. Quincy started his car and slowly drove off.

Since coming to Philly he had put in a lot of work. Now Knuckles was Face's next enemy and Quincy couldn't wait to eliminate him.

CHAPTER 92

When Knuckles walked into the office and closed the door Agents McDonald and Powaski were both waiting for him.

"Anything new?" McDonald asked.

“Same ol' shit. The streets are dry without Face's drug supply. There's a few small timers selling drugs, but nothing major. Here," Knuckles said going into his pocket and taking out a small piece of paper. He passed the paper to McDonald and said, "That's all their names and the places they sell their drugs," he grinned.

"Good job. We'll look into it," McDonald said, as he put the paper inside his shirt pocket.

"So, don't nobody know you're working with us, do they?" Powaski asked.

"Hell no! If they did, I would be a dead man! A lot of people still love Face. If anyone ever found out that I was doing this I would have to move my girl and two kids out of Philly," Knuckles replied.

"Well, don't worry, Gary. We'll keep you out of harm’s way. You just keep providing us with info from the streets and you won't have nothing to worry about," Powaski assured him.

"Did you ever find out anything about that guy, Que?" Knuclkes asked, curiously.

"No, not yet. But we're still looking into it."McDonald said.

"I told y’all that he from California," Knuckles replied.

"Still, that's not enough. We need at least a first name. Can you get that for us?," Powaski asked.

"I'll try. But like I told y’all before, I never called Que. He calls me. And he don't talk much when he do."

"Just wait for him to call you. And when he does, try and start some bullshit conversation and see if you could get him to tell you his real name. Use the recorder we gave you," McDonald

said.

"I will, but first he has to call. And Que ain't called me in weeks."

"If this guy, Que, is as ruthless as you said he is, then we need to get him off the streets fast. But, so far, we don't have anything on him. No photos and no real name, just the name Que and the description you gave us," McDonald said.

"I'm telling y'all, the guy is a cold blooded killer and he'll do anything for Face. Anything!" Knuckles said sincerely.

Do you know anybody he killed?" Powaski asked, folding his arms across his chest.

"No, not personally but I heard he killed a handful of people that were going to testify against Face at his state trial a few years back."

"Do you got any proof?" Powaski asked. "Cause there was a local prosecutor that was murdered."

"No, I don't have no proof. It's just something I heard on the streets," Knuckles told him.

Agent McDonald reached into his jacket pocket and pulled out a white envelope. "Here, this yours. We'll see you next week," he said, passing Knuckles the envelope.

"Keep bringing us good news and you'll be well taken care of," Powaski told him.

Knuckles smiled and put the envelope inside his jeans pocket and stood up from the chair. After shaking both agent's hands he left the office. A big smile was plastered on his face as he walked into the empty elevator. No one knew, not even the Feds, that Knuckles was playing both sides. Not only was he working as a paid informant for the FBI, but he was still involved in illegal activities.

Since Face's arrest Knuckles had been secretly making a lot of money selling drugs. And he was using the FBI to help get rid of all his competition. When Knuckles walked out of the federal building, a dark gray Lexus LS pulled up and he quickly climbed inside. He leaned over and kissed his beautiful girlfriend, Tameka, while their twin sons played on the backseat. She smiled and drove down the street.

Later that evening...

Inside Veronica's bedroom she and Judge Marino laid across the bed. After their second round of hot blissful sex they were both exhausted. Veronica rolled over and placed her head on his hairy chest.

"You enjoy yourself," he asked, already knowing her answer.

"Always," Veronica said in a soft whisper. "Remind me to write the Viagra company a thank you letter," she said, and they both laughed.

Veronica looked into the judge's eyes with and said, "Anthony, I need to talk to you about something."

Seeing the seriousness in her eyes, he sat up on the bed.

“What is it, Babydoll?"

"Anthony, do you know a man by the name of Norman Smith, Junior?"

His eyes widened and he said, "Yes, I'm presiding over his federal trial that's coming up soon, why?"

"Because, he's my nephew," she said with concern.

"Your nephew? Are you serious?"

"Yes, Anthony, I'm dead serious," she replied.

"Veronica, I'm sorry, Babydoll, but your nephew is in a lot of trouble. And I mean a lot!" the judge said.

"I know what's going on Anthony, but what I need to know is if can you help him?" Veronica asked.

He looked deep into her worried eyes and said, "Babydoll, I'm truly sorry, but there is nothing I can do to help your nephew get out of the mess he's gotten himself into. His case is one of the biggest cases I ever had and there's a lot of powerful people involved."

Upset Veronica said, "so you can't do nothing? My nephew was set-up and I'm sure you know it already."

Anthony reached over and grabbed her hands. "Veronica, I can't get into details about the things I know about your nephew's case. All I can tell you is this, it don't look good for him at all. And there's a lot of powerful people that need it to stay that way."

Veronica got out of the bed and grabbed her silk robe. After she put it on and tied it around her slim waist, she looked up at the judge and said, "Anthony, we're finished. Leave my

money on the dresser before you leave.

Before he could respond, Veronica turned around and walked out of the bedroom.

After the judge got dressed, he walked down the stairs and saw Veronica sitting on the sofa. "Please, Babydoll, don't do this. I love you and I don't want us to end like this."

Veronica looked up at his weak expression and said, "Anthony, you don't love me. You lust for me! If you really loved me, then you would try and help out my nephew!"

"But I can't! You don't understand how big this case is," he said.

"And I don't care! You're his judge, Anthony! You are in control of everything that goes on in that courtroom. So don't tell me you can't," Veronica vented.

Anthony got down on his knees and reached for her hands.

"Don't touch me!" she told him.

He paused and then stood up, "Why are you doing this, Veronica? What we have is special," he said sadly.

"You mean what we had was special!"

"So then, this is it? I won't be seeing you anymore?" Anthony asked, with his eyes wide and his heart pounding inside his chest.

"No, you won't be fucking me anymore, if that's what you're asking. But you will be hearing from me. And that I can promise," Veronica said, as she stood up and walked over to

the front door. "Now please leave!" she said, opening the door.

Without another word, Judge Marino sadly put his head down and walked out the house. Veronica slammed the door behind him.

CHAPTER 93

One week later...

Veronica spoke with all of her politically connected friends about helping Face at his upcoming trial, but no one was willing or able to help. She learned that Face's case was a lot bigger than what it had originally appeared and powerful people behind closed doors were secretly pulling strings to see Face go down.

Sitting in the passenger seat of Veronica's S-600 Mercedes, Pamela watched as Veronica pulled over and parked her car.

"I have one more person to see," Veronica said, before she got out of the car.

"Who?" Pamela asked curiously.

"The Mayor."

Pamela watched as Veronica walked across the street to the historic City Hall building. When she disappeared from sight, Pamela sat back and waited.

After getting off the elevator, Veronica walked over to the desk where an attractive young black woman was working at her computer.

"Yes, how may I help you?" she asked with a pleasant smile.

"My name is Veronica Taylor, and I'm here to see the Mayor. We have a meeting for one o'clock," she added, glancing at her gold Rolex.

"Hold on Miss Taylor, I'll have to check and see if he's ready to receive you," she said as she picked up the phone to announce Veronica.

Veronica stood there watching as the woman spoke into the phone. When she hung up she looked up at Veronica and said, "Miss. Taylor, the Mayor is ready to see you. His office is the black door on the right."

"Thank you," Veronica said, then turned and walked away.

When she approached the Mayor's door she tapped it lightly and stepped inside. Sitting behind his desk was Mayor Charles Klein. He smiled widely when Veronica closed the door and walked over to his desk. Her face showed of importance as she sat down in an empty chair.

"What was so important that you couldn't wait until next week to see me?" Charles asked.

"My nephew," she replied.

"Who is your nephew?" he asked curiously.

"Norman Smith, Junior. You might have heard of him by the name of Face."

Charles stood up from his desk and walked around it. When he stopped in front of Veronica's chair, he looked down at her and said, "that guy is the biggest drug dealer in the country!"

Charles, he's my nephew and I came here to see if you could do anything to help him. "

Charles shook his head and said, regretfully, "I'm sorry Veronica, but there's nothing I can do for your nephew. Me or anyone else for that matter. I'm sorry."

Veronica stood up from the chair and looked Charles in the eye. "He was set up Charles, and you know it! And now your Godfather, C.W. Watson is trying to ruin him!"

Charles's eyes widened and he said, "Veronica, the Feds want him awfully bad. They want to use your nephew as an example for all the low life drug dealers. I'm very sorry, but there is nothing I can do about it. My Godfather is a very powerful man in D.C., and he's the man behind it all."

"Can't you talk to him?" Veronica asked.

Charles laughed and then said, "He's the head of the Domestic Anti-Drug Commission. It's his job to take people like your nephew down. "

"He was set up Charles! And your Godfather is trying to ruin him just to boost his own political career!" Veronica vented.

"Even if you're right, there's still nothing that can be done about it. Your nephew has a high-profile case and there are a lot of people that's..."

"That's what?" Waiting to see him convicted and given a life sentence?" Veronica said, cutting him off in mid sentence.

Charles didn't respond, he just watched as Veronica turned and walked over to the door. She paused, then turned back around and said, "don't bother to call me anymore. You can't satisfy my needs, so why should I continue to satisfy yours?"

"Veronica, please don't do this! We go back to many years," he begged.

"Evidently all those years we had don't mean shit!"

"That's not true, Veronica and you know it!" Charles said, as he walked over to her. “Please Veronica, it would kill me if I couldn't see you anymore," he said honestly.

"And it would kill me if my nephew went to prison for the rest of his life!"

"But..."

"Save the buts, Charles! You said what you had to say," Veronica said grabbing the door knob. "This is far from over, Mr. Mayor! You'll be hearing from me again very soon," she added before she opened the door and walked out of his office.

When Veronica got back into the car she looked at Pamela and said, "Just like all the others! He can't do a damn thing to help us! So, you know what that means?!"

"Are you sure you wanna go that route?" Pamela asked.

"We don't have another choice," Veronica replied as she started her car.

"Okay, then. Plan B it is," Pamela said with a smile on her face.

Later that night...

Tasha was sitting on the bed reading some documents she had brought home from the job. Even with all the recent drama surrounding her, the T&F Real Estate firm was still doing extremely well. Isuri walked into her mother's bedroom and joined her on the bed. "Baby, what are you doing up?" Tasha asked, as Isuri snuggled up under her.

"I couldn't sleep," she replied in her innocent young voice.

"Tasha put her paperwork down and reached out and pulled Isuri into her loving arms. After kissing her on the cheek, she said, "Why can't you sleep?"

"Because."

"Because what?"

Isuri looked into her mother's eyes and said, "Because, I miss Daddy. And I keep thinking about him. Mommy, does Daddy still love me and Norman?" she seriously asked.

Tasha smiled and said, "Baby, your father loves both of y'all."

"Then why don't he come home no more? Is he mad at us?" Isuri said, as her eyes filled with tears.

Tasha wrapped her arms around Isuri and said, "Baby, your father loves you and your brother more than anything in this world. I told you that he's a little busy right now. That's all."

"But when will he come back home?" Isuri asked, as tears began to fall down her beautiful little face.

Tasha got silent, because she was unable to answer Isuri's question.

"Huh, Mommy? When is daddy coming back home?" she asked again.

"I...I don't know, Baby," Tasha said, as her own tears started to drop from her eyes.

F.D.C. Philadelphia...

Inside his quiet cell, Face laid back on the bunk staring at a photo of him and his family. With each passing day, he miss them even more. Still, he knew he had to stay strong-not only for himself, but for them as well. After putting the photo back under his pillow he looked out of the window. The dark sky was filled with stars. As he stared at them his mind began racing with thoughts. He still couldn't believe how so much had changed in such a short time, and how so many of his former friends had crossed him. In the silence of his single cell, Face stared out the window a single tear fell from his eye.

CHAPTER 94

Early July, one week before the trial was to begin...

The jury selection process lasted for three tedious days. But after questioning and evaluating over a hundred potential jurors, thirteen were finally seated; twelve jurors and one alternative, in case one of the twelve became sick, killed, or otherwise unable to continue the trial. These twelve people would ultimately decide Face's fate. Even after their long days selecting the jury, Gloria visited Face every evening and went over every small detail for his upcoming trial.

As Face sat back reading some important paperwork, Gloria sat in her chair staring at him. She couldn't help but admire his masculinity and determination.

"Did you read the statement from the person who's name is blacked out?" Gloria asked.

"Yeah, I read it when you first gave it to me a while ago," Face replied as he closed the folder and handed it back to her.

"He's one of the informants that's working for the government, but he won't be testifying at your trial, because the Feds don't want to expose his true identity."

Face smiled at Gloria and said, "They already did. They just don't know it."

"So, you know who this person is?" Gloria asked in a shocked voice.

"I know who all my enemies are. Even the ones who smile in my face," he replied.

"Do you mind telling me this person's name?"

Face folded his arms across his chest, and with a stern look he said, "Just read the newspaper tomorrow morning. You'll figure it out yourself."

Later that night...

Inside Veronica's bedroom she and Pamela sat in the middle of the pile of video cassettes and discs. They were reviewing the footage and making duplicate copies.

"Here's the list of everyone we'll send a disc to," Veronica said, passing Pamela a white sheet of paper with names and addresses on it. "So, when do you want to start sending

them out?" she added.

"When the time is right," Pamela grinned.

Veronica reached down on the floor and picked up three discs. "Here, Pamela. These are the Masters. Make sure you take good care of these."

"Don't you worry, tomorrow morning I'm going straight to my bank and put them in my safety deposit box. They'll be safe there," Pamela said assuredly. "I still can't believe that Charles confessed to you. Do you think he was telling the truth? He was drunk when he told you the story," she added.

"I don't know, but one thing's for sure, we'll soon find out," Veronica said as she placed another disc into the video player. "If what Charles' confession is the truth, and what happened in West Virginia really happened, then Face has a real big chance of winning his case."

"Yeah, but if Charles's drunken confession was false, then Face will end up in a lot more trouble," Pamela seriously said. "And even if what Charles said is the truth, it will only bring Face a lot more enemies. And you too," she added.

"You think I care? As long as we have these masters there's nothing that anyone can do to us. It's not my fault they couldn't keep their mouths shut and their dicks in their pants," Veronica

said laughing.

Pamela looked at her friend and just smiled. She knew that Veronica was a woman that lived on the edge and played by her own rules. In the privacy of Veronica's bedroom the two women sat back and prepared to watch another one of Veronica's secret sex tapes.

Southwest Philly, 78th and Linbergh Avenue...

Quincy pulled over and parked his tinted black Dodge Magnum across the street from a two story house. After screwing the silencer onto his .9mm he took out his cell phone and dialed a number. "Yo, who dis?" a man's voice answered on the second ring.

"It's me Que. What's up Knuckles?"

"Hey Que, what's up, my man? It's been a while since you called. Is everything cool?" Knuckles said, as he climbed out of bed with his girlfriend Tameka. "Is Face alright?"

"Yeah, he's cool," Quincy said.

"I see they got him in the newspapers almost every day. I really hope he beats it," Knuckles said, as he walked out of the bedroom and quietly closed the door.

"I need to holla at you about something. You got a minute?" Quincy asked.

"Yeah, anytime. Where you at?"

"I'm right outside your house. Come open the door."

"You outside!" Knuckles replied in a shocked tone.

"Yeah, I was in the area, so I decided to swing by for a minute. Is that okay?"

"Yeah, it's cool. I'll be right there," Knuckles said, ending the call and closing his cell phone. He quickly rushed back into the bedroom and put on his jeans, sneakers and tee shirt.

As Tameka laid peacefully sleeping in bed, he reached under the mattress and pulled out the mini-tape recorder. He pushed the small red record button and slid the recorder into his pocket, then he left out of the room and rushed down the stairs. When he reached the front door, he took a slow deep breath, then opened the door.

"Que, what's up my man?" he asked, as he let him into the house.

As soon as Knuckles shut the door and turned around, Quincy already had his loaded .9mm pointed at his head.

"Killing snitches. That's what's up!" he replied, squeezing the trigger five times. 'Tht! Tht! Tht! Tht! Tht!' Five near silent and deadly bullets entered Knuckles' face and chest.

When his lifeless body slumped to the floor, Quincy walked to him, stood over his body and... 'Tht! Tht! He shot him two more times in his face. Then he bent over, went into Knuckles' pocket and found the small tape recorder. He stood up and angrily shook his head. Then, he aimed the gun at Knuckles' face and shot him once again.

Quincy turned from Knuckles' corpse and walked over to the stairs. When he reached the top of the stairs he walked to the front bedroom and quietly opened the door. Tameka, Knuckles' attractive, light skinned girlfriend, was peacefully sleeping under the cover.

Quincy approached her with his gun aimed at her head. With no hesitation he squeezed the trigger two times. 'Tht! Tht!' He watched as her body twitched, then got totally still. 'Tht!' he shot her once more in the head before he turned and walked out of the bedroom.

When he walked down the hallway he stopped at the first bedroom he came across and opened the door. Two young boys were sleeping peacefully in separate beds. They were Tameka and Knuckles' four year old twin sons.

Early the next morning...

Inside a crowded Starbucks, Gloria sat at a small table sipping her Swiss Mocha Cappuccino and staring at the front page of the Philadelphia Daily newspaper. She couldn't believe her eyes. The front page headline read, 'FBI INFORMANT AND GIRLFRIEND FOUND MURDERED INSIDE THEIR HOME'. After reading the entire story Gloria had an unbelievable look on her face. She thought about what Face had told her and just shook her head. The only good thing about the tragic story was that the killer, or killers, didn't harm the dead couples' four year old twin boys.

CHAPTER 95

The trial;

THE UNITED STATES OF AMERICA VS. NORMAN SMITH, JR...

Inside the gray brick and dark oak walls of the Federal Courthouse located in downtown Philadelphia, Norman 'Face' Smith, Jr., also known as BLACK SCARFACE, was on trial for his life. Face had been charged with conspiracy to buy over 2000 kilograms of cocaine and 250 kilograms of pure heroin. He had soared to the top of the FBI's Top Ten Most Wanted list, and

the Department of Homeland Security, including the DEA and the ATF(Alcohol, Tobacco, and Firearms), were in complete agreement with the FBI's assessment.

Now, they were all here in the courtroom that was filled to capacity. Extra security had been provided by the U.S. Marshal's office, as well as two impeccably dressed, silent and stern faced white men from the Department of Homeland Security. They were the kind of men that permitted everyone around them to know something out of the ordinary was taking place. Silently, they studied everyone and everything. The government was attempting to make sure Face went away for the rest of his natural life and they didn't want anything to get in the way.

The tension in the courtroom had become palpable. Face calmly sat beside his attractive female attorney, Gloria Jones. He wore a black silk, Armani suit and a pair of black alligator

skin shoes. In sharp contrast, sitting beside the man who epitomized fear and power, sat Gloria, clean and perfect in mind, body and soul. As beautiful as Gloria was, she was an even better litigator. She worked her way up from the bottom to become one of the finest criminal defense attorneys in the nation.

Gloria shuffled through some of her most recent notes, ignoring the insanity of all the chaos around her. Face sat calmly before his judge and jury as if he were immune to their desires and intentions. He looked over his right shoulder and saw the two beautiful women that had meant more to him than anything in this world; his mother, Pamela, and his wife, Tasha. They both waved and gave him a comforting smile.

Seated right behind them were some of his good friends; Veronica, Passion, Peter J. Greenberg and White Chocolate, plus many more folks were scattered throughout the courtroom.

As Face sat back scanning the crowd, he also noticed a few of his long time enemies; Detective Ron Perry and the two FBI Agents, Jeff McDonald and Steve Powaski, to top the list. They sat staring with evil eyes and only God knew the hatred that rested inside their hearts.

Surrounded by photographers, journalists and reporters from as far away as London, the trial of THE UNITED STATES OF AMERICA - VS- NORMAN SMITH, JR., began.

Assistant U.S. Attorney, Vincent L. Bradley opened with a long winded story of corruption, violence and murder, that seemed to allege that Face was a 'mastermind' criminal and the root and cause of every problem in America.

As the twelve jurors intently listened with wide and curious eyes, various expressions of anger, outrage, fear and contempt, played across their faces while Mr. Bradley weaved his tale. It was easy for them to see and believe that as far as the government was concerned, Face was the epitome of evil.

Pictures of grisly murders, videos, and diagrams were all paraded in front of the courtroom as part of Bradley's shock and awe campaign. And while each of the spectators hung on to every piercing word that flowed from his silver tongued mouth, like it was honey from the hive, Face seemed strangely removed from Bradley's razor sharp accusations.

Face sat quiet and still, only occasionally reaching for his water glass, or to whisper something to Gloria. Watching Face, it was easy to tell that he was completely unaffected by what Bradley was selling to the men and women inside the courtroom. All of it was a circus-act that barely held Face's interest.

Vincent Bradley walked over to the twelve members of the jury and dramatically paused. After a long sigh, he turned towards Face and pointed, "Ladies and Gentlemen of the jury, that man!, Mr. Norman Smith Junior, also known as 'Black Scarface', is a mastermind criminal!," he all but yelled out.

"Mr. Bradley, this courtroom is not a stage, therefore your theatrics is uncalled for. Let this be a warning," Judge Marino interrupted.

"I'm sorry, Your Honor," he replied in a tone that indicated he couldn't care less about this courtroom. It was his stage and he was going to shine when he got a chance! "His multi-faceted organization is responsible for the cold blooded murders of State Prosecutors, lawyers, police officers, rival drug dealers, innocent women and children, and anyone else who got in his way to the top! Please don't be fooled by his calm nature. That man sitting there," he continued to point, "is a ruthless criminal that I intend to expose to everyone inside this courtroom!"

After Mr. Bradley finished his opening statement, it was Gloria's turn. Though she stood only five feet and five inches tall, in the courtroom she was a giant. She had mastered the

art of vocal inflection to get the most revealing reaction from a jury or a witness. With a single glance she was able to completely disarm the most vicious prosecutor the government had to offer.

To date, this was the biggest case of her career. It was known as a career maker, or a career breaker. She knew that the stakes were astronomically high, but she was prepared to

offer the very best defense.

Gloria stood up from her seat and looked around the stunned courtroom. After Mr. Bradley's opening statements she decided to take a slightly different approach. She calmly approached the twelve jurors and pleasantly smiled, and took the time to make eye contact with each and every one of them. She applauded their courage for agreeing to take part in this trial, praising their ability to look at all the facts involved in the case, and thanked them, in advance, for not making decisions based on theatrics.

Gloria spoke to the jurors as if they were her brothers and sisters. As she spoke to them, Vincent Bradley slouched more and more from each word that came out of her mouth. She didn't try to attack any of the government's evidence. Rather, she explained how the government has the ability to 'come up with' and 'create' evidence to fit any person or crime they wanted. She pointed at the jurors one by one telling them that any one of them could be in Norman Smith, Jr.'s position.

She went on to paint a vivid picture of harassment and dishonesty; dropping little details along the way about the jurors lives...details that she received from her own private investigators. She might say to the jurors some analogy about being a waitress and having somebody steal your tips, knowing full well that two of the jurors were waitresses.

There was something for all of them. Gloria wasn't fighting the prosecution, she was slowly developing friends…comrades against the over-reaching power and viciousness of the machine; Big Brother! The United States Government! She would worry about fighting the case's particular elements one witness at a time. But, in her opening statement she just wanted thirteen new friends; 12 jurors and 1 Federal judge.

CHAPTER 96

Three weeks later...

For three weeks the prosecution brought in a few evidential witnesses to build their mountain of evidence against Face. These included two of the arresting officers, a DEA agent, and an investigator from the U.S. Treasury department. Gloria cross examined them, doing the best she could to subtly call their integrity into question. She had a way of making a witness doubt himself and his evidence, even when he was a so called 'expert'. It wasn't as much as what she said, but instead, it was the way she said it.

As for Face he had remained calm and collective throughout all the proceedings. Every day he walked into the crowded courtroom dressed in a brand new suit and a pair of alligator skin shoes, waving and smiling at his family and friends. He was a man who refused to let his enemies see him sweat or break under pressure. Some people would call it being 'cocky' or 'arrogant', but anyone who really knew him associated his demeanor with confidence.

With all the national media attention that the trial received, Face became known as somewhat of a celebrity. And every day, it seemed like a new website was popping up on the internet sensationalizing him and the case. Because of his handsome looks and 'bad-boy' image, Face was growing quite popular with women. It had turned into a media circus, exactly what the government wanted, to expose Face and his criminal organization to all of America.

After Judge Marino called for a brief recess, Face was escorted to a small holding cell in the back of the courtroom. As he sat on the bench waiting for the trial to resume, Agents

McDonald and Powaski approached the cell. Face looked at the two agents and smiled.

"Laugh now you son of a bitch, but you're going down!" Powaski said. "And then we'll get the last laugh when you're ass is doing a life sentence in federal prison!"

Face didn't respond to the agents threats and goading. Rather, he just sat there grinning the entire time.

"We know you had something to do with Knuckles and his girlfriend being killed. You might fool all your female admirers, but we know you're nothing but a low-life thug! And

sooner or later all of your games will come to an end!" McDonald fumed. "You're a cold hearted coward and I hate everything you stand for!" he added angrily.

McDonald reached under his shirt and pulled out a loaded glock .9mm. He aimed the weapon at Face's head and said, "I should kill your ass right now!" he threatened.

Face sat there calm and unflinching. He never blinked.

When McDonald heard someone coming from behind them, he quickly put the gun back under his shirt.

"Is everything okay here?" Gloria asked as she approached the cell with one of the court's deputies.

Face calmly stood up from the bench and walked over to the cell door, "Yeah, Gloria, everything is just fine here. These nice agents came by to tell me how much they like my new

suit," Face said with a big grin.

Gloria and Face watched as the two agents angrily turned and walked away. She knew that there was a lot more to it, but she refused to ask him about it.

After Face was released from the holding cell, he and Gloria were escorted back into the courtroom.

Later that evening...

After another long tedious day at trial, Gloria returned back to her elegant suite at the Ritz-Carlton Hotel. Today had been another verbal battle with U.S. Attorney Vincent L. Bradley, and she was relieved that it was finally over. After taking a hot soothing shower, she put on her panties and a long white tee-shirt. Then she called her husband back at home in New York. After a brief conversation on the phone they said their 'I love yous' and hung up.

Gloria laid back on the big comfortable bed. Her laptop, cell phone, and a small stack of legal paperwork were lying right beside her. She knew that tomorrow would be another

long and drawn out day in court. She also knew that she would have to cross-examine the government's list of 'expert' witnesses that were prepped and ready for their day at trial.

So far the trial wasn't turning out to be anything like she had planned. The government did everything it had to do to win its case. And deep down inside, Gloria felt as if she

were trapped inside the middle of a losing battle, but she refused to back down and throw in the towel. Not only was Gloria fighting in the case of her life, but she was secretly fighting for the man she still deeply loved and cared about.

After a brief rest she sat up and placed the laptop between her legs, moments later she was back at work, typing on the keyboard, getting herself ready for another long day at trial.

Washington, D.C...

"Vincent, you're doing a wonderful job. And like I promised you, after the trial you'll be greatly rewarded for your work," C.W. Watson said into the phone.

"Thanks Senator. So far, things are looking in our favor. And I haven't even used our key witness yet. Tomorrow morning I'll be bringing in the FBI's top voice specialist.

He has all the documents to verify that the two voices on the FBI's recorded conversation is indeed Roberto Chevez and Norman Smith, Junior. And there is no way that the defense can get around it," Vincent said with excitement.

"Good work, Vincent!" C.W. said as he stood from his desk and walked over to look out the window. "How about when this is all over, we suit up and go do a little hunting?"

"I would really like that, Sir. Just let me know when you're ready," Vincent replied with a smirk.

"I sure will. Besides we'll need some time to talk alone. Especially about the new position you'll be getting," C.W. said as he stared out the window. "Just continue to keep me updated on everything that's going on in the trial."

"I will, Sir. I'll call you tomorrow evening. Take care."

"Goodbye, Vincent," C.W. said before closing his cell phone.

After a sigh C.W. turned from the window and walked back over to his desk. He grabbed his jacket and black briefcase then headed for the door.

Once he was outside of his office, he smiled as he walked down the long empty corridor with the sounds of his footsteps echoing down the hall.

CHAPTER 97

Over a month had gone by and now the government was finally ready to bring in the first of their four key witnesses. In prior weeks, the government had brought in a long list of expert witnesses to help them with their case. And Gloria was ready for them all. Every time the government would put one of their expert witnesses on the stand, Gloria would counter attack with a cross-examination.

With every new day, the case became more and more intense. On a few occasions Judge Marino, had to pull both lawyers to the side and warn them about their verbal insults. The trial

had turned into a personal battle. And now so much was on the line that neither one of them wanted to be on the losing end of what was surely the biggest case of their lives.

All of the whispers that were going on inside the courtroom came to an abrupt stop when the doors opened. Every eye in the room was focused on the government's witness, Roberto Chevez. Dressed in a pair of khaki pants and a white polo shirt he slowly walked forward. Every step he took was visibly more unsteady than the last. At any moment he expected someone to appear from the crowd, with a gun and mow him down. As he walked, his eyes nervously darted back and forth. He noticed a man in a black shirt that looked strangely out of place. He continued the uneasy walk toward the witness stand and breathed a sigh of relief when he approached it. Looking back into the crowd, the strange man was no longer there.

Before he knew it, his right hand was raised and the bailiff was swearing him in. As he sat, Vincent Bradley approached him with a look of confidence.

"Can you please state your full name for the record and so everyone in the courtroom knows who you are?"

"Roberto Chevez," he said, as he leaned into the microphone.

"Mr. Chevez, can you please tell us what you do for a living?"

Roberto answered just like they had practiced many times, "I made my living as a narcotics trafficker for the Gomez drug cartel."

"And where is the Gomez drug cartel located?" Mr. Bradley said as he turned away from the witness stand and looked at the jury.

"Nicaragua," Roberto stated.

"Mr. Chevez, in your business dealings did you ever come in contact with Mr. Norman Smith, Junior?"

"Yes, all the time," Roberto answered.

"Is he present in the courtroom? And if he is, please point him out?"

"Yes, that's him. The black guy in the nice suit," Roberto answered dropping his shoulders, as he raised his hand and pointed an accusing and trembling finger directly at Face.

There were a few chuckles around the courtroom, and Bradley continued to ask question after question. By the time it was all said and done the courtroom was completely silent. Roberto

had spilled his guts. He talked about the inner workings of the Gomez drug organization and explained how the whole process worked, from the farmers who grew the coca plant and how they processed it and made it into the finished product. On maps, Roberto pointed out where the coca plant was grown in Nicaragua and he told the routes that were taken to fool the DEA and customs agents when the drugs were smuggled into the United States. He went into detail about the distribution network that was in place in the United States and how drugs were turned into lots of money. Lots and lots of money! He even went as far as explaining how drug proceeds were laundered.

The testimony of Roberto Chevez was like a nuclear bomb to the defense. So much damage had been done that Gloria just shook her head, turned to Face and said four words, "That really hurt us!"

When Mr. Bradley had finally finished questioning the witness, he walked back to his seat with a big smile plastered all over his face. With Robert's statement, Gloria knew her task had become that much harder. Since the start of the trial his testimony was the most damaging.

In her brief cross-examination, Gloria attacked Roberto's character. She also exposed his motive for testifying against Face. Her cross examination skills were powerful and poignant. Still, deep inside her soul, Gloria knew that it wouldn't be enough. Roberto Chevez's testimony put Face in a deeper hole and Gloria knew it would take a miracle to pull him out of it. What was even worse for the defense, the government still had three additional key witnesses prepared to testify against Face.

After the trial had ceased for the day, everyone left the courthouse. Two U.S. Marshals escorted Face back to the Federal Detention Center, while all of his family and friends sadly got into their cars and headed for their homes. When Face entered his cell he walked over and sat down on his bunk. His mind began to race with thoughts as he reviewed the day's developments. Roberto's testimony made his chances of winning the case so much more difficult. And Face knew that things weren't looking good for him.

Then, an image of Roberto Chevez entered his mind and a big smile came across his face. Like always, Face was two steps ahead of his enemies. Roberto Chevez's slap in the face would be nothing compared to what Face had planned for him.

Chestnut Hill...

Inside Pamela's beautiful new home she and Veronica sat on the couch and was totally engrossed in a serious conversation.

"We gotta send the letters and the disc out, now!" Pamela said, as tears fell from her eyes. "Roberto Chevez really hurt Face's case in court today," she added.

Veronica reached out and grabbed Pamela's trembling hands. "Okay, Pam, I'll start getting everything ready," she said tearfully. "Lord, I hope this don't backfire," she added.

Pamela stared deep into Veronica's watery eyes and said, "The only way to find out is to send them. Right now my son is in a lot of trouble and it don't look as if things will be changing anytime soon. The discs are all we got. Now, we just gotta pray that they help'em and don't hurt'em!"

When Veronica left the house, Pam watched as she stepped inside her Mercedes and drove off. After closing the door she sadly walked over and sat back down on the couch. As she

thought about Face, tears of hurt and pain escaped from the confines of her hazel eyes.

Downtown Philadelphia...

Quincy was waiting outside the entrance/exit tunnel, where law enforcement personnel traveled through the secure parking garage under the courthouse. He knew that at any moment an armored plated, Lincoln Town Car would leave with two FBI agents in the front and one, Roberto Chevez, tensely sitting on the back seat. He figured the only vehicle leaving would be

the Town Car with Mr. Chevez in it, because he had just finished giving his testimony.

Quincy knew the vehicle, because hours earlier, he had waited and saw the Town Car when it first arrived at the Federal Courthouse. He remembered Mr. Chevez looking like most other 'snitches' on their way to testify; nervous, anxious, scared and confused.

Some static came over Quincy's walkie-talkie and then a static voice said, "One here. What's up?"

Quincy put the walkie-talkie to his face and said, "stand by for a minute. They comin'."

As the words escaped his mouth, the dark gray Town Car slowly pulled out and drove in the flow of traffic. It turned right, and proceeded down a one way street.

"I got 'em! It's a dark gray Lincoln Town Car. License plate number, USG-372. Give them three or four blocks and then box them in."

"One here," a voice said. "I'm passing you right now. I'll stay on his bumper."

"Two here. I'm one block south. Let me know if he turns," a deeper voice said.

"Three here. I got the east covered."

"Four here. I got the west."

Quincy nodded proudly to himself. The four tinted vans were waiting in every direction, there was no way the Feds could escape the 'hit-teams' net.

"He's going east! He's going east!" a voice said.

"Three here, I see them. I'll jump a couple of cars behind."

Quincy was making his way slowly back through traffic, relying on his men to be his eyes. "Okay, listen," he said carefully. "Don't get on their bumper. Wait until four and two catches up. You guys know the drill."

Three blocks later the Town Car passed a McDonald's restaurant and an old looking van slammed on the breaks in front of them.

"Goddamnit!" Agent Guthrie barked. "Son-of-a-bitch just locked his brake!"

Sitting beside him, Agent Jackson was cussing after spilling his diet 7-Up down the front of his shirt. Sitting on the back seat, Roberto Chevez was so scared that his complexion was almost pale white. He couldn't even speak when the brown van pulled up and boxed them in on the right side.

"What's going on?" Agent Guthrie said, as a blue van blocked the left side so tight that they couldn't open the doors. As the agents started furiously reaching for their weapons another van hit them from behind. "Call it in! Call it in!" Agent Jackson yelled frantically, and reached for his radio.

Suddenly a tinted black Bonneville pulled up and a man with a ski mask quickly rushed out the car. He climbed on the hood of the Town Car with a pistol in his left hand and a white

index card in his left. Agent Guthrie was trying to use his cell phone because the radio was full of static. His phone wasn't working either.

A frequency jammer in the back of the green van made sure the agents couldn't make any calls.

"Relax," Agent Jackson said, as he gripped his Sig-P228. "The windows are all bullet proof. They can't shoot through them."

"Pinche idiots!" Roberto screamed. "They're here to kill me. That's the man with the black shirt! Face sent him kill to me!"

"They're just trying to scare us. That's all" Agent Guthrie said, trying to calm their witness.

The man on the hood leaned towards the windshield, and tapped on the glass with the tip of his H&K

USP .45. When he was sure he had their attention, he placed the file card in front of

them, pressing it against the windshield.

The note read, 'Mr. Chevez, hopefully God will forgive you, because we won't. By the time you finish reading this note, five pounds of C-4 Semtex will have been affixed to the bottom of this vehicle in the form of a shaped charge. Now would be an appropriate time to pray.'

The man slowly climbed off the hood, got back into his car and closed the door. With a worried look, Agent Guthrie read the note. He turned toward his partner just as the flash went off, instantly flooding the Town Car with hot flames and dark smoke. The armored vehicle proved to be good at keeping bullets on the outside, but not as good with the high-explosives .

The vans dispersed, each going their separate ways, and drove into the darkness of the night while the flames were still scorching Roberto Chevez and the two federal agents to cinders.

Inside the tinted Bonneville, Quincy pulled off his ski mask. Hearing the loud screams of the three dying men was like music to his ears! As he pulled off and drove down the street, he heard the loud explosion behind him and the glimpse of a smile appeared upon his face.

CHAPTER 98

The next day...

The tragic news about the murders of Robert Chevez and the two Federal Agents had spread through the city like a wildfire. From the crime ravaged streets of North, West and South Philly, to the elegant Chestnut Hill section, with its broad tree-lined streets and multi-million dollar homes. Everyone was talking about it, even the national media covered the story. Because of all the excitement surrounding the case, Judge Marino decided to postpone the trial for a week. The case was beginning to take its toll on everyone; from the pawns and knights, to the bishops and the kings who maneuvered behind their walls of secrecy.

Washington, D.C...

"Vincent, what the hell happened?" C.W. fumed into the phone.

"Mr. Wilson I don't know what to say but I can assure you, Sir, that the FBI and the local authorities in Philadelphia are thoroughly investigating the case. Whoever was behind these

murders knew the vehicle and the exact time the witness would be transported from the courthouse. They were waiting for them," Vincent said into his phone. "And now, because of our flaw, a witness and two FBI agents are dead."

C.W. stood from his chair and walked over to the window. It was something he did four or five times a day . He stared out into the calm summer sky as he spoke into his cell phone.

"Vincent, I want you to bring this man down! I want him ruined! You hear me?" C.W. vented.

"Yes, Sir, don't worry. I will! We still have three other key witness that have yet to testify. They're all due to take the stand once the trial resumes."

"You just make sure that the rest of the witnesses are heavily guarded at all times. I don't want what happened yesterday to ever happen again!" C.W. said solemnly, then turned around and walked back to his chair and sat down.

"Don't worry, Sir. It won't! You have my word! And sooner or later we'll find the culprits responsible and they will all be brought to justice!"

After Vincent Bradley closed his cell phone he reached for and picked up the Philadelphia Daily Newspaper that was laying on his desk. The bold, black headline read: FEDERAL WITNESS AND FBI AGENTS BURNED ALIVE INSIDE VEHICLE!

"Face, you're going down, you son-of-a-bitch!" Bradley mumbled, as he quickly dialed another phone number.

Inside the Federal Detention Center, in downtown Philadelphia...

Face and his personal financier, Peter J. Greenberg sat beside each other in the visiting room.

"Peter, did you get the other money from my wife?" Face asked.

"Yes, Face. It's already deposited and collecting interest with all the rest. I told you, my friend, that everything will be taken care of. You just win this case so you can enjoy all of it," Peter said, sincerely.

Face looked at his friend with a pleasing smile. "Just remember to split everything between my mother, wife and children if anything was ever to happen to me."

"Don't you worry, that's already been taken care of. I told you when we first met years ago that I would take care of you. And that the rich know how to hide their assets- just leave everything up to me," Peter said, with a prideful smirk.

"Thanks Peter," Face said, as the two men stood from their chairs and shook hands.

"I'll be back to see you soon. Take care," Peter said before he turned and walked away.

As soon as Peter disappeared Gloria Jones entered into the visiting room with an intense look upon her face. With her briefcase in her hand, a C.O. escorted her and Face into a smaller inmate/attorney visiting room. When the door closed and they were left alone, Gloria looked straight into Face's eyes and said, "Face, I need for you to call off your goons. We don't need this trial to be any harder than it has to be!"

Face leaned forward and grabbed Gloria's arms in a tight grip. His voice dropped to an angry whisper, "Gloria, you do your job…And let me do mine!"

Gloria stared into Face's eyes. She felt fear and was turned-on at the same time. The man who stood in front of her was unlike any other man she had ever known. And Gloria knew that the only rules Face played by were his own.

West Philadelphia...

On the corner of 52nd and Girard Avenue, a tinted dark red Ford Expedition pulled up and parked. Detective Ron Perry got out of his dark gray Toyota Camry and rushed over to the truck.

When he got inside, Agent Jeff McDonald pulled off. His partner, Steve Powaski was sitting in the passenger seat an both of them looked somber.

"So, what's so important fellows?" Ron Perry asked, as he relaxed into the back seat.

Agent McDonald pulled up and parked the truck near the corner of 48th and Lancaster Avenue, right across the street from the old cemetery. After he cut the engine off he turned

toward Ron Perry and said, "We need you to do us a very big favor."

"What is it?" Ron Perry asked.

"We want you to kill Face!" Powaski replied, his blue eyes dead serious.

"What? Are you serious?" Ron Perry asked, leaning forward in his seat.

"Dead serious! That no good son-of-a-bitch is responsible for two of our finest men getting killed yesterday and Roberto Chevez. Now he needs to pay! And life behind bars just ain't good enough!" Agent McDonald vented.

Ron Perry sat back and smiled, "when would you like this done?"

"Soon. When the time is right…we'll let you know. So, is it a deal, or not?" Powaski asked.

"Y'all have yourselves a deal," Ron Perry said, as he reached over the seat and shook hands with both of the agents.

"And don't worry, Ron. This will be between us only. We'll get you everything you will need. Just when it's time, don't miss the target," McDonald said.

"Don't worry. I never miss!" Ron Perry grinned.

On the ride back to Ron Perry's car they discussed a few small details. Ron Perry was excited beyond words. The FBI had secretly hired him to kill the man that he hated more than anything in this world. His trigger finger already itched with anticipation.

After Ron Perry had climbed into his car and pulled off, Agent McDonald drove off in the opposite direction. When he stopped the truck at a red traffic light, he looked at his partner with a devilish grin and said, "so far, so good. I'll call Mr. Bradley and tell him that our pawns are in place." After Face is found guilty he won't be going to prison. He'll be going directly to his grave!" he added.

"Then one of us will have to eliminate Detective Ron Perry," Powaski said wickedly.

When the light changed, McDonald drove through the traffic light and looked at his smiling partner and said, "Since I took care of the last two pawns, Ill leave this one up to you."

Agent Powaski beamed with excitement, knowing that Detective Ron Perry was a dead man walking and he would be his Grim Reaper!

CHAPTER 99

One week later…

When the trial resumed a new witness was introduced to the crowded courtroom. Dressed in a pair of faded blue jeans and a white sweat shirt, Vernon 'Truck' Wilson was escorted into the courtroom by one of the court deputies. After taking the stand he was sworn in by the bailiff. Truck sat down with a apprehensive look. For months he had been nervously waiting for this day to arrive. A few times he had changed his mind and decided not to go through with it. But, the thought of getting back his freedom was just to strong to ignore and the government made him a deal that he couldn't resist. Still, deep in his burning soul, Truck knew that he had violated the ultimate code of the streets; to never snitch! Now, this former drug boss was one of the key witnesses testifying against Face: the same man he had brought into the drug game nearly ten years ago.

Face stared at his former friend with burning eyes. The pain inside of him was tearing at his crying soul. As Truck sat on the witness stand being questioned by the U.S. Prosecutor, Face sat calmly in his chair. Occasionally he would reach for his water glass, take a sip, then listen as Truck sat there spilling his guts.

Truck sat on the stand giving the court an Oscar worthy performance. Crying, laughing, and pleading to his captivated audience. He told the court everything he knew about Face,

and more. He told them about the first time they met, and how Face and Reese were his top two street enforcers. He also let the court know about the drug money he gave Face to start his

illegal business, and all the checks he received from T&F Real Estate Firm, that was owned by Face's wife, Tasha.

The twelve men and women of the jury sat there in complete awe. The jury listened on as Truck cried when he told them about his favorite nephew A-Rock, and his girlfriend Foxy, and how he suspected that Face and Reese were responsible for their murders.

Looks of total disbelief was written across the jury's shocked faces. A few jurors were even in tears. Before the Prosecutor finished questioning the witness, Vernon 'Truck'

Wilson had painted a picture of the most violent gangster to have ever existed; a man that was so ruthless he would kill anyone in his path.

"He's a monster! Face is a man who won't hesitate to kill for money or power!" Truck shouted into the microphone.

Face sat back. When he glanced over his shoulder, he saw that Pamela and Tasha were both in tears.

"You killer!" someone shouted out loud.

"Order in the court!" Judge Marino said, as he banged his gavel down hard. "One more outburst like that, and you'll be escorted out of here!"

Face sadly turned around and folded his arms across his chest. The sight of seeing both his wife and mother cry, almost brought him to tears as well.

As Gloria stood from her chair to cross-examine the witness, the entire courtroom was completely silent. With all seriousness, she leaned over and whispered in Face's ear, "Don't worry, Face. I'm gonna expose this fraud". Then she stood straight up, fixed her eight hundred dollar Gucci outfit and headed toward the witness with an air of confidence. She was ready for war!

Gloria approached the witness stand and started clapping her hands, "your performance was very good, Mr. Wilson. Unfortunately, not everyone in this courtroom was fooled," she said. "So, let's not beat around the bush. Let's get straight to the point, shall we?"

Truck sat on the stand trying to look as comfortable as he could but underneath his calm exterior, there was a very nervous man.

"Mr. Wilson, is it true that you were once a major drug dealer in West Philly?"

"Yes," Truck spoke into the microphone.

"Is it also true that you were set-up by your nephew in an undercover-sting operation?"

"Yes," Truck replied, looking a little confused.

"Is it true that the same nephew that set you up and got you a twenty-five year sentence was also sleeping with your girlfriend, Foxy?" Gloria asked, walking toward the jury's box.

"Yeah," Truck mumbled.

"I can't hear you, Mr. Wilson. Can you please speak up?

"Yes!" Truck barked.

Gloria turned and walked back over to the witness stand. She looked at Truck and noticed that sweat beads had started to form on his forehead. "Mr. Wilson, is it true that for testifying here today, you'll received a major reduction on your federal sentence?"

"Huh? I...I..."

"Just answer the question, Mr. Wilson."

"Objection Your Honor! The witness..."

"Objection overruled!" Judge Marino said, cutting the prosecutor off in mid-sentence.

"So, will you be receiving a major time cut? You know, 'A get out of jail free card'?" Gloria said, as a few people started laughing.

Truck's eyes were stretched wide and his forehead was covered with sweat. He looked at the Prosecutor for some type of moral support…anything to help him get out of answering the question.

Gloria waited patiently, watching as her nervous witness squirmed on the stand. At the same time the twelve members of the jury looked on with thought-provoking eyes. Seeing Truck's body language had exposed his weakness.

"I, I was promised a deal if I told the truth," Truck finally answered.

Gloria laughed and said, "And it takes that long for you to tell the truth?"

Once again there were a few laughs from the crowd and from some members of the jury.

"Either the truth really hurts, or you're just one big liar," she told him. "So let me see…you were set-up by your own nephew, the same nephew that was having a secret affair with your girlfriend. You received a twenty-five year sentence for trying to buy twenty kilos of cocaine from an undercover FBI agent, and now you're here in court today testifying against your former friend so you can get out of prison, and put him in! The same friend that made sure you never needed a single dime while you were doing your time in prison. You said it yourself, 'once a month a check was sent to you from the T&F Real Estate Firm'," Gloria said, as she faced the crowd. "Mr. Wilson, while you were away in prison, did anyone else send you any money?"

"No," Truck answered sadly. "Just Face," he added.

Gloria smiled and just shook her head, "So, this is how you do your friends?"

"Objection your Honor!" Bradley said, as he stood from his chair.

"Objection overruled!" the judge said.

"I...I'm...sorry Face," Truck said, putting his face down in total distress.

"If everything you said was the truth, Mr. Wilson, then why should you be sorry?" Gloria asked sarcastically.

After a few more personal questions Gloria had Truck in tears, catching him in lie after lie.

Bradley was squirming in his chair, watching helplessly as Gloria was easily breaking down one of his key witnesses. He was furious.

When Gloria had finally finished questioning Truck, she calmly walked back to her seat and sat down.

As she whispered something into Face's ear, the crowd, Judge, and jury all sat there completely stunned; Mrs. Gloria Jones had impressed all of them.

CHAPTER 100

After Gloria's powerful cross-examination, Truck was escorted out of the courtroom by the Court Deputy. Once out of the court room, he was immediately surrounded by four heavily armed U.S. Marshals. The four Marshals escorted Truck through a secret tunnel that led straight to a small private parking lot. When they all reached the parking lot a tinted, black armor plated Chevy Suburban was parked and waiting. Two more U.S. Marshals were standing around, pistols cocked and ready for anything. This time the Feds were well prepared; they had cars stationed all along the route they were to travel. When the Suburban pulled out the parking lot, Truck sat on the back seat with his head down. As his mind raced with thoughts a single tear fell from the corner of his left eye.

Later that night...

Tasha was laying back on the sofa enjoying the sounds of Jill Scott. She had just finished listening to Mary J. Blige and Keisha Cole, two of her favorite singers. In the tranquility of her home she let the smooth music take her far away, to another place and another time...

October 1993...

Seventeen year old Tasha rushed through the front door in tears. She had just been in a fight with one of the girls at her high school. Her long black hair was all over her head and partly covered her face. She had light red bruises on her neck and face. Momma watched as Tasha sat her backpack down on the floor and walked over toward her. She grabbed the remote control and turned the TV off. With a smile, Momma looked into Tasha's watery eyes and asked, "Did you win?"

Through falling tears Tasha managed to show a smile, "Yes Momma, I won", she said whipping her tears away.

"Good, cause if you would've lost we were going right back out there, so you could fight 'til you won," Momma honestly told her. "Now, tell me what happened?

Tasha looked deep into Momma's caring eyes and after a deep sigh, she said, "Momma, I had to beat up some girl that was all up in Face's face. Her name is Stacy Robinson and she's

been liking him for a while. I saw them standing out in the yard talking and I just snapped!"

Momma reached over and grabbed Tasha's hands. "Tasha, you can't keep beating up every girl you see talking to Face. He's a handsome boy, and there's a lot of little girls that's

gonna like him. What did Face do while you were fighting this girl?"

"He pulled me off of her and told me to go home," Tasha replied.

Momma smiled and shook her head. She knew that her young granddaughter was deeply in love, and no one, not even her, could change the way Tasha felt about Face.

"Momma, he drives me crazy, and sometimes I don't know what to do!" Tasha said, as the tears started to fall. "I don't know why I love him so much!" she cried.

Momma leaned over and wrapped her loving arms around Tasha's back. Tasha laid her head on Momma's breast and tearfully sobbed. "I'm...I'm afraid Momma," she muttered.

"Afraid of what, Baby?" Momma said, as she tried her best to console her.

"I'm afraid that one day some other girl is gonna' take Face away from me. "

"Look up," Momma told her.

Tasha looked up at Momma's genuine £ace.

"That boy love you more than anything in this world. Trust me, Face is going nowhere. You got a hold on his heart forever," Momma said, then leaned forward and kissed Tasha on the lips.

"Thank you, Momma," Tasha said producing a big comforting smile.

When Tasha woke from her memories, she sat up and looked around the empty living room. As Jill's soulful voice floated out of the speakers, Tasha laid back down and let the tears escape the confines of her eyes.

CHAPTER 101

One week later...

Another week had passed. Now Gloria and Face were both prepared for the government's final two witnesses. So far the trial had been a seesaw battle. Still, with all the evidence and witnesses the government had, Face and Gloria both knew that the cards were stacked high against them. And with the last two witnesses that were waiting to testify, things didn't look as if it would get any easier.

Inside the Federal Courthouse...

The crowd of onlookers silently watched as the deputy led one of the government's star witnesses to the stand. After Jose Gomez was sworn in, he calmly sat down and looked out at all the staring faces. He didn't want to be there, but he felt he had no choice. It was simple; either he testify against Face, then go into the Federal Witness Protection Program, or he spend the rest of his natural life inside a maximum security Federal prison somewhere.

When the federal prosecutor walked over to the stand, he got straight to the point. "Can you please state your full name for the court?"

"Jose Manuel Gomez," he said into the microphone.

"And, Mr. Gomez, can you tell everyone here where you are from?" Mr. Bradley said, as he paced the floor.

"I am a citizen of Managua, Nicaragua."

"And can you please tell the court what you do for a living?" Mr. Bradley said with a smirk on his face.

After clearing his throat, Jose put his mouth to the microphone and said, "I am an international drug trafficker."

"And what type of drugs did you traffic?"

"Cocaine and heroin," Jose said, showing no signs of nervousness.

"And where are some of the places you took these drugs?"

"All over the world. Including here in the United States."

Mr. Bradley walked over near the jury stand and paused, " And how much of these drugs did you smuggle into this country?"

"Tons! Many, many tons," Jose answered.

"Did you have any help moving and getting rid of so much contraband?"

"Yes, I supplied many people to help my cartel move the product."

"Mr. Gomez, can you look around this crowded courtroom and find anyone that you supplied with drugs?"

Jose pointed to Face and said, "Him. Right there. Norman Smith, Junior."

Some commotion came from the back of the courtroom and Judge Marino silenced them when he banged his gavel. "You may proceed," he told the prosecutor.

"And around how much drugs did you supply for Mr. Smith?"

"Too much to count. All I know is Face was me and my brother's top man. And we supplied him with enough drugs to run eight major U.S. cities."

"Wow! I'll bet that was a lot," Bradley said, being melodramatic. "You mean to tell this court that one man had that much respect and power, to be put in charge of eight American cities?"

"Yes," Jose replied. "He was the best!"

"The best, meaning what, Mr. Gomez?"

"That there may never be another drug dealer like Face, ever again. He is a man who is in a league of his own," Jose said, honestly.

"So, you really think so?"

"No, I know so. That is why he was my top man."

Mr. Bradley walked back over to the stand and stopped directly in front of Jose. "Mr. Gomez, are you saying that Mr. Smith is one of the biggest drug dealers in the country?"

Jose smiled sincerely and said, "No,..."

"Objection! Your Honor, leading the witness!" Gloria shouted, coming to her feet from behind the defense table.

"Objection overruled," Marino stated dryly. "Please answer the question, Mr. Gomez."

"What I was saying is that, considering the amount of drugs Mr. Smith was moving, he was by far the biggest drug dealer in America!"

"Objection, your honor. Supposition. The witness has no proof that he was the biggest smuggler bringing drugs into America. Therefore, his testimony has no basis for his claim. It's merely a personal belief and therefore prideful boasting."

"Overruled. Based on the amount of drugs in question, Mr. Gomez's opinion may, in theory, be a fact!"

For almost three more hours Jose Gomez sat on the stand telling the shocked crowd and jury everything he knew about Face and his violent drug organization. Just like Roberto Chevez

had done weeks earlier, Jose painted a vivid picture of corruption, murder and mayhem, and blamed it all on Face. His powerful testimony was a lot worse than what Roberto had done. This

was the 'Boss' himself. One of the two leaders of the Gomez drug cartel telling the world that Face was a cruel, heartless drug kingpin and how he was a man who yearned for power, and

wouldn't hesitate to kill a single soul that stepped in his path.

Gloria sat back listening, occasionally looking over at the hypnotized jury to see their reactions. She could tell that most of them had already made up their minds. And so could

the smiling prosecutor.

Two days later, Jose's younger brother, Rico Gomez took the stand. Just like his brother had done he too told the story of a violent and ruthless drug kingpin called Norman 'Face' Smith, Junior. Their stories were almost identical.

Once again Gloria had done a powerful cross examination but still she felt that it wasn't

enough. In his closing arguments, Mr. Bradley reminded the jury that Face had been one of the biggest, if not the biggest, drug dealer in U.S. history. A ruthless, cold blooded killer with a violent temper.

"Norman, 'Black Scarface' Smith, Junior, is the epitome of pure evil," he told the jury. "If we ever plan to save this great country from all the evils that exist, then I pray that we start right here!"

When it was Gloria's turn for her closing argument she told the jury about a loving husband and father of two young children. She told them about a passionate man who had four

non-profit charities that helped poor inner city children stay away from drugs and guns. She told the jury how Face was a high school graduate with a spotless criminal record. And how

all of Face's money came from his wife's multimillion dollar real estate company.

Gloria painted a picture of a loving, caring man that wouldn't hesitate to give a friend the shoes off his feet and the shirt off his back.

"Norman Smith, Junior, is a person, just like you," she said, pointing to the jury, then around the courtroom. "He knows what it's like to grow up in the ghetto, fatherless and poor. He knows what it's like to see his loved ones die and to struggle, and only want the very best for his family. Norman Smith, Junior is not the monster that the government would like for you all to believe he is. Look at him." Gloria pleaded.

All eyes in the courtroom turned to study Face.

"Does that man look like he is responsible for all of the destruction in America? When the facts show that our government is the cause of most of the pain throughout the world. Do you all see those two women crying behind him? That is Norman's lovely mother and beside her is his wife. Think about being in their shoes and hearing all the lies being told about the person you

love. Ladies and Gentlemen of the jury, today you can fix what is broken; a system that is designed to destroy its own citizens. I close my argument with something that Norman once told me. He said, "Jealousy is love's worst enemy."

When Gloria looked around the courtroom, she saw lots of understanding faces. The crowded courtroom was in complete silence.

She walked back to her chair and sat down. She had done her very best, and Face couldn't ask for more. Now, the final decision was left to the twelve members of the jury. It would be their job to decide if Norman Smith, Junior would go free, or spend the rest of his life in prison.

CHAPTER 102

Two days later...

The Jury was still deliberating and had yet to come up with a unanimous verdict that would decide the fate of the accused. In the meantime, Face was in his cell at the Federal Detention center, patiently waiting the outcome. The last two days felt more like two years, but Face remained calm and poised. He read his favorite newspapers, exercised, called Tasha and his children and occasionally he wrote a few letters. At night before he went to bed he would get down on both knees and pray to God. In the tranquility of his cell he would confess his sins.

As Face laid across his bunk reading the Philadelphia Inquirer's newspaper he had no idea that he was in the midst of a world of political chaos.

Downtown Philadelphia...

Inside his private chambers, Judge Marino sat back watching the sex disc featuring him and his young black mistress, Veronica. A terrified look was on his pale white face. The footage was

clear enough for anyone to see that it was him. As he watched with wide eyes, he couldn't believe it.

An hour earlier, he picked up the small package from his secret P.O. Box Address. He knew that the package was from Veronica, because other than himself, she was the only person who had the address. As the judge nervously watched the explicit footage, he reached into the opened package and took out a small white postcard. Dubiously, he stared at the card. It read: If Face loses, then so do you!

Judge Marino turned off the disc player and removed the small disc. After putting the disc and card inside his jacket pocket he quickly reached for the phone. When he dialed the number, he realized that he had never been this scared in his entire life.

City Hall...

Inside his elegant office, Mayor Charles Klein reached for the remote and turned off the DVD player. He stood from his leather chair and nervously started pacing the floor. After watching the sex disc with him and his long time mistress, Veronica, he knew that his political career was now hanging in the balance. He had watched the disc three times and each time he cringed and slouched in his chair.

The confession that he made on tape was enough to destroy him and his godfather, C.W. Watson's, political careers. Worried, Charles rushed over to his desk and sat down once again. He looked at the small white post-card that was in his trembling hand, 'If Face loses, then so will you! He couldn't believe that Veronica was blackmailing him. But, it was true and he couldn't do anything about it.

Charles reached into his jacket pocket and took out his Blackberry cell phone. First he started to call Veronica, but her line was no longer in use. She had gotten all of her old phone numbers changed a day earlier. After a long sigh, Charles dialed another number and nervously waited for someone to pick up the phone.

"Hello Charles, it's good to hear from you," C.W. Watson said, answering the phone. He had seen Charles' name on the caller ID.

"Godfather, I need to see you. It's very important!"

"What is it? Tell me now!" C.W. said.

"Not over the phone. I have to see you in person. I'll meet you at home later tonight," Charles said before ending the call and closing his cell phone.

As he sat in his chair staring at the white postcard, Charles was filled with total fear. He confessed his deepest and darkest secret and it was all caught on tape. Now the lives of so many people were at stake.

Inside the U.S. Attorney's office, downtown Philadelphia...

Vincent Bradley and FBI agents Jeff McDonald and Steve Powaski sat at a small conference table talking.

"I have some good news, fellas'. The jury is leaning towards a unanimous guilty verdict. I found out through my inside source," Vincent said with a grin. "My good friend, the court

deputy has been transferring information to me straight from the Jury Foreman himself," he added.

"Did you talk with Mr. Watson?" Agent McDonald asked.

"Yes, I told him the good news earlier today and he's just as excited as I am. Face is going down!"

"And then, six feet under!" Agent Powaski said as they all laughed.

Vincent's expression quickly changed to a more serious one, "Don't no one but us three and Ron Perry, know about the 'hit' on Face. I would like to keep it that way."

"Don't worry, Mr. Bradley. After Face is found guilty our pawn will put a bullet in his head. Then he will receive one the same way," Powaski said in all seriousness.

"There's no better way for a vigilante, crooked cop, to kill his long time enemy. The press will eat it up! And no one will know that the government is behind all of it!" McDonald said.

"I can't wait. Face is responsible for the deaths of a lot of good agents. Now, it's his turn to meet his demise," Powaski replied.

"I have some more good news, "he said.

"What is it?" McDonald asked curiously.

"After the verdict is read and Face is found guilty, I'm resigning from my job as the U.S. Prosecutor."

"What?" Powaski asked excitedly. "Are you serious?"

"Yes, I'm very serious," Vincent replied.

"But why?" McDonald asked.

"Because I'll be moving my family to Washington, D.C. to prepare for my new job," Vincent grinned.

"And what will that be, Sir?" Powaski asked.

"A member of future President Watson's executive staff," Vincent replied. "He's already promised me a job."

Chestnut Hill, Philadelphia...

Veronica pulled up and parked her Mercedes in front of Pamela's house.

"By now, everyone should have received their packages and we'll find out very soon if our plan worked or not," she said to Pamela.

"I'm gonna tell Face what we done when I go visit him later. He needs to know what's going on," Pamela said.

"Alright, just call me later tonight," Veronica said, as she leaned over and gave Pamela a kiss and a hug.

After Pamela got out of the car and went into the house, Veronica took her tinted Gucci frames off the top of her head, put them on, and drove away.

Inside the Federal Detention Center...

Face had just left from mail-call and returned back to his peaceful cell. After he closed the door, he sat on the edge of his bunk and started looking through the large stack of mail; mostly letters from his friends and family.

When he saw the name Sandy Carter on one of the envelopes he pushed all the other letters aside. It had been a while since he had last received mail from her. But, the letter wasn't from Sandy. It was actually from his best friend, Reese.

Since Face got arrested, they used Sandy to correspond with each other through the mail.

Face ripped open the envelope and took the letter out. After he got comfortable on his bunk, he unfolded the paper and began reading Reese's handwritten letter;

"Dear Face, when this letter reaches you I hope that you're in the best of health and spirits. What's up, Homey? I been reading about the case and seeing your face on the news. Everywhere I look, I see they're talking about the case. Please stay strong and keep praying to God. As for me, I'm staying out of trouble and staying very focused. I'll be out in a few years and you know once I touch down, it will be on again! A real hustler can't be stopped. Ain't that what you always used to tell me?

Anyway I got some more news to tell you. A few months back the 'pigs' came here and had the nerve to ask me to testify against you. I couldn't believe that shit! They threatened me and told me a bunch of bullshit about doing life in the fed, or living free in a federal witness protection spot if I snitched you out. I just listened to the pigs as they explained how bad they wanted you. Then one of the pigs had the nerve to ask, "Would Face do life for you?' On the outside I just frowned at the dickhead, but on the inside I was laughing my ass off. I knew right then and there, that they ain't have a clue about the man they were dealing with. Or me.

About a week or so later, the pigs showed back up and the C.O.s came and got me out of my cell again, (you know I was pissed off!)

Face smiled as he continued to read...

Anyway, this time when I met up with the pigs I rammed on they bitch asses! I told them stupid mutha-fuckers that I ain't no snitch and I would rather die from a bullet to the head than to snitch on my best friend!

After they left I never seen or heard from the pigs again. Anyway, I just wanted to keep you posted on what was going on. Other than that everything is the same ole' same ole'; doing

my time and not letting my time do me. I'll keep praying for you, Homey. No matter what the outcome, I'll always be your right hand. Love Reese."

P.S. I never forgot what you used to tell me; "Blood is thicker than Water. But, Love is thicker than Blood! You were never wrong!"

After Face finished reading Reese's letter, he put it back inside the envelope. With a single tear falling down from one of his eyes, he smiled and shook his head.

Later that night, Bethesda Maryland, a small suburban town on the outskirts of Washington, D.C...

Inside the basement of his lovely two story home, C.W. Watson paced the floor furiously. He and his god-son, Charles, had just finished watching the sex tape. On the secretly made sex tape, Charles had made a drunken confession about the tragic event that had happened more than 35 years ago. Still, the confession was enough to destroy both of their political careers forever. And C.W. Watson knew that if the sex disc, with Charles' confession on it ever got into the wrong hands, he would never reach his dream of becoming the next President of the United States.

"What the fuck were you thinking about?" he paused and shouted.

"Godfather, I'm terribly sorry! Please forgive me!" Charles begged.

"Sorry? My chance at the White House is now in the hands of this black nigger whore that you were fucking! Now, all you have to say is that you're sorry?" C.W. fumed.

"I was drunk... I didn't know what I was saying," Charles cried out.

C.W. walked up to Charles and reached out and grabbed his shirt collar, "You stupid son-of-a-bitch! You fucked everything up! Now, I have to make some important phone calls and try to fix this fine mess you put us in!" he vented.

"Please forgive me Godfather! Veronica was setting me up the whole time and I never knew it" Charles said, as his eyes welled with tears.

C.W. stared at Charles in disgust. "I can't believe you let a woman trick you like this. Especially a Black one!"

C.W. released his grip and watched as Charles sadly lowered his head. As he went back to pacing the floor, he still couldn't believe what had happened. How his own godson had

put him in a desperate situation.

"Damn!" he snapped.

Charles was too scared to look him in the eye, so he shamefully kept his head down and his eyes focused on the floor.

C.W. took out his cell phone and dialed a number. He knew that if he didn't act fast then his time would run out. As he waited for someone to answer the phone, the words on the

postcard flashed in his head; 'If Face loses, then so will you!'

CHAPTER 103

Early the next day, outside the Federal Courthouse...

Vincent Bradley stepped out of the black limousine and closed the door. He had an incredulous look on his face. The news he just received was the most disturbing he had ever heard; there was a major problem, and the powers that be were counting on him to help fix it.

Vincent walked toward the two waiting Agents and pulled them to the side. Seeing his distraught expression, they could tell that something was terribly wrong.

"What's up Mr. Bradley?" Agent Powaski asked.

After a long sigh Vincent looked at both men and said, "Call everything off!" he said in a demanding voice.

"What?" Agent McDonald asked as if he hadn't heard him correctly.

"You heard me! Call everything off!" he repeated angrily.

Both agents knew that it wouldn't be wise to question the Prosecutor's authority. He had given them a direct order and they had to obey it.

Agent Powaski angrily took out his cell phone and impatiently dialed a number.

All three men stood around waiting as it continued to ring. "He's not answering his phone," Powaski finally said.

"Well, where the hell is he?" Vincent barked.

"We're not sure, Sir. Last night after we gave him the weapon and getaway car that he was supposed to use, he told us he would call us this morning. But so far he hasn't called. Or answered his cell phone," Agent McDonald said. "But, we'll keep trying until we reach him."

"You do that! Things have gotten out of hand, and that cop could make matters a lot worse! So, find him!

And find him fast!" Vincent said, then turned around and angrily walked away.

The two agents watched as Vincent Bradley walked up the courthouse steps and entered the building. "I wonder what's going on?" Powaski mused, as they walked to their parked car.

"Whatever it is, I'd bet it has something to do with the limo parked over there," McDonald said, pointing to the tinted, black limousine.

"Let's go find this fool. I don't want the person in that limousine mad at me," Powaski said, as they both climbed inside the car.

One hour later, Bala Cynwyd, Pennsylvania...

The all white Mercedes Benz pulled up in front of the beautiful Spanish style home. An attractive blond haired woman pressed the horn twice. Moments later Peter J. Greenberg walked out of the house carrying a large black briefcase. He walked over to the car and climbed inside. After placing the briefcase on the back seat, he leaned over and gave the woman a long and zealous kiss.

"You ready to get out of here?" she asked with a big grin.

"I've been ready. Our plane is waiting at the airport," Peter said, as he relaxed in his seat and folded his arms across his chest. "I just heard over the radio that your friend's trial

has resumed. They're going to read the verdict today," the woman said, pulling off. "What do you think the verdict will be?"

"From what I saw, the government can't lose. They had so much evidence and too many witnesses testified against him. Two of them were bosses in one of the world's largest drug cartels."

Wow, that really sucks!" the woman said.

It's funny how your friend today could be your enemy tomorrow," Peter said.

"You're funny," the woman said stopping the car at a red light. "Do you want to hear the verdict? They're going to broadcast it live over the radio?"

"No, it will be depressing. I just want to get on that plane and get as far away from this country as possible," he said seriously.

"Sounds good to me. I can't wait to sunbathe on the nude beaches of Costa Rico," the woman said, as they continued on their way when the light turned green.

Inside the Federal Courthouse...

The trial lasted a laborious two months. Each day seemed longer and more intense than the previous day. Today, the final scene of the final act of this dark and dreary affair would come to a end and the curtain would fall. Whether or not there would be an encore was yet to be seen. Today the long awaited verdict would be read. Today, finally perhaps, justice would be served. The expectation and the curiosity, the tension and dread was as thick as a London fog rolling through the courtroom in roiling sheets. One could almost taste it.

'It shouldn't be long, now,' Gloria thought, glancing up at the clock on the far wall. They'll be back any minute.'

Her mind bounced back and forth like a pinball machine, considering the possibilities as she briefly glanced across her shoulder at Face. He was so remotely calm and relaxed. She briefly wondered if he was even human. She wondered how anyone could totally distance themselves from all of this. She put some papers back into her black leather briefcase that were lying on the table in front of her. As her fingers swept across the gold medal clasps she noticed a slight electric shudder pass through her body; from the tips of her pink painted toenails to the very crown of her head. A tinge of nervousness and anxiety shimmered through her entire hourglass figure.

Face glanced casually around at all the people in the crowded room. His glance said that this was nothing but a circus to him; nothing more. The faces of family, friends, enemies, victims, Federal agents, reporters and spectators were tense and dreading. Some smiled with satisfaction and excitement, waiting to see the black king go down. But what really caught his eye was seeing the expression on Prosecutor Vincent Bradley's face.

For a few seconds they just stared at each other. Face could sense a feeling of pure hate coming from him. Bradley was being forced to do something he was in total disagreement with and could have never imagined. Something so unthinkable that if it didn't get done, the lives

of so many powerful people would be ruined forever and he would be to blame.

Suddenly, the jury room door opened. The twelve men and women who made up the jury, of his peers, calmly filed out and made their way to their assigned seats. They did their best not to make eye contact with Face, Gloria, and Bradley, but a few snuck a peek. They had deliberated for three long days and now however, they were ecstatically relieved to be finished.

In fact, they were giddy with relief. Now they could all get back to their normal lives and stop living in this surreal world where drugs, money, murder, power, greed and secrets ruled the

hearts of men; a world and lifestyle that was impossible for them to understand and tolerate. But it was now over! The United States of America -VS- Norman Smith, Jr. would finally come to an end for once and for all.

CHAPTER 104

Agent McDonald pulled over and parked on the corner of 8th and Chestnut Street. He glanced at Powaski, who had his cell phone to his ear. "He's still not picking up!" Powaski said angrily.

“Fuck! Where the hell is that fool?" McDonald barked.

Powaski closed his cell phone and said, "We have to find him fast, before he does something stupid and get us all killed!"

McDonald slammed his hand down hard on the steering wheel, his anger rising with each passing minute. "Just keep calling him! He has to pick up sooner or later!" he said.

Powaski dialed Ron Perry's cell phone number again and waited while it continued to ring. After a long sigh, McDonald started up the car and pulled away from the curb. He knew that if they didn't find Ron Perry soon, a lot of people would be in big trouble, him included.

Right across the street from the Federal Courthouse, Ron Perry was situated on the roof of a small fast food restaurant. He had been there since five o'clock that morning, patiently waiting for his golden opportunity to arrive.

After the two agents had dropped off the rifle and the getaway car at his house and left, Ron Perry left a short time later to get into position. He had gotten into the getaway car and placed the rifle in the passenger seat, then he headed toward downtown Philadelphia to find the perfect sniper 'hide'.

After searching around the back of the building he found a fire escape and climbed onto the roof. Once there, he knew that it would be the perfect position to fire from. He found a place in a corner where he could see the whole street, but no one would notice him. He sat there with his headphones on and the rifle across his lap. He was listening to the trial that was being broadcast on live radio. A few feet away from him was a bottle of spring water and a bag of barbeque potato chips. His cell phone was laying next to the bag.

Occasionally Ron Perry would stand up and look over the roof's ledge and down at the street below, watching as cars and people went up and down the street. He saw the black limousine parked right outside the courthouse and wondered who it could be. The limo had been parked there for hours. He knew that whoever it was, they were someone important because the police officers that patrolled the area outside the Federal Court Building, left the limousine completely alone.

As Ron Perry sat back waiting for the long awaited verdict to be read he had no idea that his cell phone had been ringing nonstop.

Camden, New Jersey...

Inside a small house, the TV was on in the living room. The voices of different CNN reporters were discussing the possible outcome of Face's nationally televised trial. Slumped

on the couch facing the TV set was special agent Jack Parker. At the kitchen table was his partner Dave Moore. They were the two agents who were responsible for the safety and well

being of the Gomez brothers until they were delivered into the Witness Protection Program. The front of both of their shirts were covered in blood. Fifteen minutes earlier both of their throats had been cut from ear to ear and the Gomez brothers were nowhere to be found.

CHAPTER 105

Clad in his black silk robe, Federal District Judge, Anthony T. Marino leaned back in his high backed, black, swivel rocking chair a bit to give his aching back a rest. He took a deep breath and closed his eyes momentarily, wondering at how he had arrived at this juncture in his life. Had fate, long ago, preordained this for him; that he would sit in judgment of a man considered to be the most vile and evil man in America? He wondered how all the people's lives had zigzagged until they had all come together here in this place, at this precise time. Fate was definitely fickle. That's a fact, he thought.

Considering all the power he had, the case presently before him had more depth and magnitude than he could have ever imagined. Now, he felt as if Satan himself sat on trial before him.

There was a great deal of attention from the press, as well as from behind closed doors, in powerful places where people trembled with bated breath and quivering hands knowing that it was possible for their dark secrets to be exposed.

Judge Marino gazed around his domain, then slowly shifted forward. His hand firmly gripped the gavel and the room became almost instantly silent; it was as if everyone had collectively stopped breathing. He cleared his throat and then spoke in a clear baritone voice that floated throughout the courtroom with ease.

"Mr. Foreman, has the jury reached a unanimous verdict?" "Yes, Your Honor. We have," the foreman replied in a high pitched, squeaky voice that rattled with stress.

The bailiff stepped over and reached for the verdict slip. The Foreman handed it over as if glad to be rid of the decision it proclaimed. Every eye in the room followed the paper from the Foreman's hand to the Bailiff's.

As he walked toward the Judge, the Bailiff glanced at the Prosecutor and gave him a slight nod. That was the sign to let him know that everything had been taken care of.

When the Bailiff handed the verdict slip to Judge Marino, everyone continued to stare at the paper as if it were some strange and exotic creature that may burst into flames at any moment.

Judge Marino leaned slightly to his left with his hand outstretched waiting for the paper knowing there was nothing in the courtroom to fear. With the slightest glance at the paper, its answer was predetermined, he sighed and shook his head ever so slightly, his face betraying not a trace of his swarming thoughts. He was a man who possessed and wore a perpetual iron gaze, keeping his true emotions deeply hidden from outsiders. Strangely though, a slight hint of a smile played at the right corner of his mouth; though it was barely visible to anyone.

After a quick glance, he handed the verdict back to the Bailiff who then transported it back to the jury's Foreman.

"Mr. Smith, please stand to hear the reading of the verdict," Marino demanded solemnly.

Face slowly rose from his chair. He adjusted his suite jacket carefully. Gloria stood beside him resting a reassuring hand on his arm.

The focus of the entire room centered on Face and Gloria, but unlike the white sheet of paper that held so much attention, people were wary of making any contact with Face; even behind his back.

He smiled inwardly knowing they were petrified and fearful of him and how he would react when he heard the verdict. Mass hysteria had infected them all.

Looks of compassion and anger and sympathy and hate wrestled their way through the room. People edged farther forward in their chairs. Then, Judge Marino nodded as he instructed the Foreman, "Mr. Foreman, would

you please read the verdict for the court?"

The nervous Foreman had sweat forming on his forehead. Perhaps it was from the gravity of the moment, or the overhead lights bearing down on him. It could have been the fact that he was overweight and under qualified for the responsibility thrust upon him. Whatever the cause, he was barely holding up under the strain of his responsibility. His nervous eyes flicked around the room, darting here and there, seeking a friendly place to focus.

In reality he was fearful of what was about to erupt inside the confined space in which he was trapped once he read the verdict aloud; which was forever irreversible. Then, he found himself staring into the dark, mysterious and alluring eyes of Face.

Face stood there not blinking and waiting for the trembling weakling of a man, who was about to announce his fate, read the verdict. Though Face stared raptly, his mind was far away; in a place where only memories thrived. He heard not, acknowledged not, the whirlwind of excitement, anticipation, fear and glee that crashed around him like the ocean's surf at high tide. He stood there reminiscing back over his entire life. Memories came in lightning flashes of good and bad...and ugly.

"Face! Face!" Gloria said, as she bumped him with her shoulder.

Face instantly snapped from out of his momentary daze just in time to hear the jury's Foreman finish reading the verdict.

"We the jury find the Defendant, Norman Smith, Junior, not guilty on all counts!" the Foreman stated decisively.

The entire courtroom went into an uproar. People were standing up in their chairs shouting, clapping and screaming Face's name, while others were standing around booing and cursing the unfair decision.

Face reached out and gave Gloria a triumphant hug. "We did it, Face! We did it!" she gasped unbelievingly as tears began rolling down her face.

A swarm of family and friends quickly gathered around them to join in the celebration. While the news reporters and photographers were trying their best to burst through the boisterous crowd for interviews and photographs.

Vincent Bradley disappointingly closed his brief-case and eased his way through the crowd. The pain that rested inside of him was worse than anything he had ever felt. He

had just lost the biggest case of his career. Not because of his arguments, they had been flawless, but because he had been ordered to do so...or else!

Judge Marino looked out at all the commotion inside his courtroom and quietly stood from his seat. As he walked back to his chambers let out a sigh of relief.

"Baby, you did it!" Tasha said, wrapping her arms around Face as they passionately kissed. "Our children miss their father. Let's go home," she added.

A group of reporters and photographers followed Face and his family out of the courtroom. Two tall white men, dressed in black suits watched quietly as they passed. Face noticed them staring, but kept walking. Serious expressions were on their faces as they stood back watching Face and his entourage of family and friends walk down the hall and straight out the courthouse doors. They made sure they stayed close behind.

Looking through the scope mounted on a Remington 700 .308 caliber rifle, Ron Perry watched as the crowd of people walked out of the front of the Federal Courthouse. He had heard the verdict on the radio and couldn't believe it. How could they let a monster like Face go free? Still, it really don't matter, Face will never live to enjoy his freedom, he thought.

Ron Perry spotted his target in the middle of the crowd. Face was surrounded by reporters, photographers and members of his family. He noticed the two well dressed white men standing just a few feet away. Ron Perry shifted his focus back onto his main target; Face. He had the cross hairs resting gently right between Face's eyes, and once he pulled the trigger it

would be an instantaneous death.

"I got chu' muthafucker! I got chu, right where I want you," Ron Perry whispered to himself.

One of the TV reporters walked up to Face and blocked the flawless line to a picture perfect shot. "Damn! Hurry up and move out the way, you son-of-a-bitch!" Ron Perry whispered urgently. Suddenly, his cell phone began to ring. He thought about not answering it until he finished the job of killing Face, but the TV reporter was still blocking his target, and the cell phone continued to ring.

"Move you son-of-a-bitch!" he begged, the phone continuing to ring and distract him from the job at hand. He started to shoot through the reporter, but thought he might deflect the bullet enough that it would miss Face and give him enough warning to get out of the way before he could get another shot off.

After a sigh he reached over and grabbed the phone and angrily opened it, "What is it?" he said furiously.

"Ron retreat. It's been called off!" Powaski demanded.

"What! I got him! Just let me finish the job!" Ron Perry barked back.

"Abort the mission! That's an order, Perry!" Powaski told him in a demanding voice.

"But, I got him! Please, I got him right now, just let me finish the job," Ron Perry begged.

Agent McDonald grabbed the cell phone from out of Powaski's hand and said, "You heard him! Now, abort the damn mission!"

Ron Perry dropped the cell phone and looked through the scope again. The TV reporter had just walked away and now the two men, dressed in black had approached Face.

"What the hell is going on, here?" Ron Perry mumbled, staring through the scope. After a long disappointing sigh, he took his eye from the scope and laid the rifle aside. He was furious

that his golden opportunity had been ruined. "This ain't over, Face! I can promise you that!" he stated aloud, as he slid the rifle into a long black leather bag.

Ron Perry reached down and picked up the ringing cell phone, "Hello!" he stated through clenched teeth.

"Don't worry, you'll get another chance," McDonald said before ending the call.

Outside the courthouse...

"Someone very important wants to see you, Mr. Smith" one of the black suited men said to Face.

"I'll talk to them later," Face said.

"That won't be a wise thing to do," the man replied. "Come on, he's waiting right over there." the man continued, pointing at the limousine.

"Face, is everything okay?" Gloria asked.

"Everything is fine," the man said, as he and his partner walked Face toward the limousine.

Face looked back at Tasha and Pamela's worried faces and said, "Just wait for me. This won't take long."

As he continued to follow the men over to the limousine, Face had a gut feeling about who was inside and he couldn't wait to meet him.

CHAPTER 106

Sitting at the curb outside the Federal Courthouse where Face had just been found 'not guilty' the long black limousine sat with its engine idling almost silently. In the plush leather back, C.W. Watson tensely sat in his climate controlled comfort. His political career teetered in the balance. His long hidden and deepest dark secret was now known by a number of people that he could in no way trust. As it now was, he had to compromise his beliefs and dedication to his position as head of the Domestic Anti-Drug Commission in order to save his reputation and that of his friend, Tom Klein and his godson Charles, the Mayor of Philadelphia. If he would have known forty years ago what he knew today, young Charles would not have left the deep wildering forest of West Virginia.

Even now, almost forty years later it was nearly impossible to believe that a simple deer hunting trip could turn into such a living nightmare. He had just laid out nearly three-thousand dollars for a custom made Winchester .300 caliber WSM bolt action rifle for the trip and he planned to use it. It seemed foolish to him to lay out that kind of money for a rifle, that wasn't yet available to the general public-and not kill a single deer with it during all of the hunting season.

He remembered that it had been the last day of the deer season and he wanted a dead deer on his fender in the worse way. He saw it as proof of his masculinity; a testament to his very manhood. Plus, being a newly elected Senator with a trophy buck under his belt, he could walk proudly through the halls of the Senate Building in Washington, D.C.

* * *

In the Fall of 1969 the early West Virginia morning had been cool and to the point of being crisp, and misty. In the wilderness valley where he had taken up a shooting position he could see through the underbrush for a fair distance. Sure, there were blind spots, but still he would know a deer when he saw one. He had been an outdoorsman all his life and was comfortable around guns, shooting and hunting.

He noticed that Tom and young Charles, were beginning to look at him with a slight smirk on their face and laughter in their eyes. That had only served to make him even more determined to show them up.

The sun had just risen over the eastern horizon and long purple shadows stretched westerly. The misty air had taken on a yellowish-silver tint and the breeze was carrying the scent of Autumn pine and wood smoke from a distant campfire. Birds had begun to chirp and flit from bush to limb in the near silent wilderness morning.

Then, a limb on a bush fifty yards out and at his two o'clock position moved more than anything except a deer could have moved it. And C.W. took aim through a hole in the bushes and waited patiently. He knew the animal would have to pass that spot on its journey east.

The crosshairs in the scope wavered slightly. His breath slowed down and his finger tightened slightly on the trigger. Then, the animal stepped from behind the next bush and filled the hole C.W. was sighted on. He squeezed the trigger and the rifle thundered and echoed through the wildering valley of West Virginia.

He heard an ear piercing scream filled with anguish. It was a gut wrenching sound he never heard before and one that he would or could never forget. He had never heard a deer scream like that! He worked the bolt, ejecting the spend cartridge and putting another fresh Silver Tip in the chamber. Knowing that the rifle was automatically cocked and ready to fire, he lowered the rifle and began to step slowly and cautiously to the site of the wounded animal. He knew that just because the animal was down, it didn't mean it was harmless. In fact, he knew it would be even more dangerous, because now it would be fighting for its very survival.

Behind him he heard noise crashing through the brush and something quickly rushed toward him. He spun around, the rifle up, level and ready to fire.

His best friend Tom and his godson, Charles came bursting around a bush and into view. C.W. cursed under his breath and lowered the rifle. His heart beat was hard and fast in his chest and his breath was trying to outrun his heart. Behind him he could hear the wailing of the wounded animal.

"Did ya' get 'im?" Tom asked breathlessly, his red face was flushed from excitement and the short run from the camp.

"Yeah, over there. He's down and wounded. So be careful. He's still real dangerous!" C.W. replied, then turned and started for his kill.

He pushed through the final bush limbs and stepped into a small clearing beside the creek. He stood there shocked, and in opened mouthed silence, as Charles and Tom pushed through the brush behind him. Then they too stopped and stared in complete quiet.

C.W.'s first thought was that he was looking at the strangest deer he had ever seen. Then he realized that what he was actually seeing was a man, lying on his back, and a woman weeping hysterically on his bloody chest. His second thought was that his political career was over if anyone ever found out what had happened here.

"Oh, fuck!" Tom mumbled, just loud enough for the woman to hear him over her hysterical and pleading cry.

The woman looked up at C.W. without raising from her hovering position and studied him through her watery, tear filled eyes. Then, her eyes dropped to the rifle he held, then back to his guilty face as realization dawned on her.

"You killed him!" she screamed through in anguish.

"Accident," C.W. mumbled. "I thought it was a deer," he explained.

"You killed him! You bastard!" she screamed. Suddenly she recognized him. "I know who you are! You're that new, young Senator! You killed him! You killed my husband!" she continued to say as she began to tremble.

"It was an accident!" C.W. pleaded, spreading his arms helplessly.

"It was murder!" she screamed back, as she wept over her husband's dead body..

"C.W. what are we gonna do?" Tom asked frantically.

"Fuck, I don't know!" he replied seriously. "This will ruin me!" he added selfishly. "My political career will be over!"

"It was an accident," Tom said, looking down at Charles, who was staring blankly at the dead man and weeping woman lying on his chest. Her face and hands were covered with blood from the man's wounds. He hadn't wanted to come anyway, Tom remembered. Now, this had happened. No wonder the kid was speechless!

"Yeah, but try explaining that to the public, Tom! They'd never buy it! Not in a million years! There's only one thing to do," he said, then took two long steps toward the woman, placed the barrel near the side of her turned head and pulled the trigger. POW! They all watched as the woman's lifeless body slumped over her dead husband.

As the echo died away the only piercing sound heard was that of the hysterical young Charles, who had fallen to his knees screaming in utter shock.

"Let's get 'em buried, Tom, and then get the fuck outta here!" C.W. said. "Take Charles back to camp and bring the shovel."

The blaring high pitched car horn beside the limousine brought C.W. back to the present. Realizing that what he had thought were Charles' screams, forty years ago, was just a car horn and nothing more. He quickly wiped the sweat from his brow using his snow white silk handkerchief and took a swallow of his iced cold tea.

Now, there was a digital, full colored video recording of a drunken Charles spilling his guts about the whole affair, and a note threatening to release a copy to the media if Norman 'Black Scarface' Smith was convicted. C.W. instantly realized that if that were to happen, then Norman Smith may be sitting in prison for the rest of his life, but he would be sitting on death row in the state of West Virginia!

His decision had been instant. He had called the necessary people, pulled the necessary strings and Norman 'Black Scarface' Smith, Jr. was a free man and was being escorted to the back door of his limousine.

As the door opened and Face slid inside, C.W. said, "I want that fucking master tape and all the copies!"

Face smiled, then said, "Senator, I just got acquitted of all charges. I know nothing about a tape."

"You bastard!" C.W. said. "You should never give a man in a high position a reason to hate you," he threatened.

"Senator, all my life I've been prepared for what I want, believe, and stand for. Are you?" Face asked.

"Is that a threat?" C.W. asked, angrily.

Face's eyes narrowed with his stoic expression. "I'll see you around, Senator. Maybe I'll call you sometime," he added, opening the back door of the limousine.

"This ain't over, Smith!"

"The name is Black Scarface, Senator. Face for short!" Face winked, then climbed out of the limousine and closed the door.

He nodded at the body guards around the limo, then walked back towards the front of the courthouse to meet up with Tasha, Pamela, and the rest of his family and friends.

CHAPTER 107

One week later...

After being acquitted at his federal trial, Face had been a busy man, running around and taking care of a lot of personal business. One of the things he had done was to go visit Reese at the state prison. They had enjoyed a long; much needed, conversation; discussing their strategies and plans for the near future. Before Face left him, he promised Reese that he would write to him and visit again in the near future.

When he wasn't taking care of personal matters, Face spent quality time with his family. His brief stay at the Federal Detention Center was one of the worst experiences he ever had. He promised himself that it would never happen again. In the meantime, there was still a lot to be done. Some former friends had crossed him and Face was determined to one day settle the score. Still, his biggest problem wasn't the former friends that had tried to get him a life sentence in prison. His major problem now was an entirely new enemy; C.W. Watson, one of the most powerful men in America.

Belmopan Belize...

Face stepped out of the, tinted black Mercedes Benz, limousine and walked through the front door of the Atlantic International Bank. This bank, where he had hidden all his money was not like any other bank in the world. Instead of tellers, floor managers, and lines of people, there was only one desk situated in the middle of the round shaped room.

Standing at the back of the room were two well armed security guards. Their demeanor made it clear that they would not hesitate to shoot on sight. Face approached the attractive, dark haired woman sitting behind the desk. He sat down in the empty seat in front of her and smiled.

"Welcome to the Atlantic International Bank of Belize. How may I help you, Sir?" she asked politely.

"I would like to check my account, please," Face replied.

"Name please?"

"Norman Smith, Junior," Face replied.

The woman paused from typing into the computer and looked up. She knew he looked familiar. Now it all made sense. It was Him! The man who had beat the U.S. government!

She smiled, then turned the computer around and shoved it toward him.

"Mr. Smith, please enter your personal access code?" she smiled.

Face typed in his personal password and code, then slid the keyboard back to the woman. He watched as she pressed a few keys and then picked up the telephone and spoke quietly into the mouthpiece. Face couldn't understand a single word she said, as she spoke in Spanish. When she hung up, she looked over at Face and said, "Mr. Smith you can go back now. The guards will

escort you."

With a smile and roaming eyes, the woman watched as Face stood from his seat and walked toward the two guards waiting at the back of the room..

The three of them boarded the elevator and as the doors began to close, one of the guards asked, "How many games do you think the Philadelphia Eagles will win this year?"

"Seven," Face answered without hesitation.

The two guards grinned and nodded their heads. Had Face answered any number other than 'seven', they would have killed him on the spot, no questions asked.

When the elevator stopped, one of the guards reached forward and entered a code into the built in keypad. The elevator doors slowly slid open and they all walked into a lavishly decorated room. The room had thick cream colored carpet and glass tables with bowls of peppermint candies and bottles of champagne chilling on ice. There were also several couches with end tables. Two more guards were inside with a tall attractive, dark haired woman who introduced herself as Sandy. When she spoke, her accent was distinctly British.

"Mr. Smith, what can we do for you today?" she asked. "I'd like to check my personal account."

"Follow me, please," she smiled, then led him over to one of several computer terminals.

"Please enter your personal account information."

Face leaned forward and started typing in his access code and password. After he pressed the 'enter' button the screen instantly changed to his personal account information. He stared

at the screen in confusion. He looked over at Sandy and said, "What the hell is going on?"

"Excuse me, Sir? Is there a problem?" Sandy asked.

"Yeah, a big problem! Where the hell is my money?" Face barked.

"Please calm down, Mr. Smith and let me see what's going she said, as she leaned over to look at the screen.

"According to our records, Mr. Smith, you withdrew five-hundred million dollars from your personal account a little over a week ago, leaving a remaining balance of twenty three million in your account."

"I was locked up over a week ago!" Face replied.

"I'm terribly sorry, Mr. Smith but the only possible way for your money to be withdrawn is if someone knows all your secured passwords and codes. And as you can see all the security precautions were followed," she said.

Face stood there with a look of total disbelief. No words could describe how he was feeling inside.

"Mr. Smith is everything okay? Would you like for me to call in the bank president?"

"No that won't be necessary. Everything is fine," Face answered disappointedly. "Sandy, do you have a piece of paper?" he asked.

"Yes, I have some right here," she replied, reaching into her pocket and taking out a black ink pen and a small white note pad. She passed them to Face then watched as he wrote down a

name and some more information. Face passed the pad and pen back to Sandy and said, "If this person ever comes back in here and uses this name, can you please notify me immediately?"

"Yes, Mr. Smith. No problem. I'll put this information in your personal records. If he comes here and uses this name you'll be the first to know," she assured him.

"Thank you," Face said.

Before he left the bank he had all of his passwords and code numbers changed. When he got back on the elevator, Sandy waved goodbye before the elevator doors closed, then she looked

over at the guards and said, "I have the feeling he'll be back in here really soon."

When Face walked out of the bank, the Mercedes Benz limousine was waiting to take him back to the airport. When he climbed inside, Tasha saw the distant look on his face and said, "Honey, is everything okay?"

Face looked into his wife's caring eyes and said, "No, but it will be and someone is gonna pay severely."

As Face sat back explaining the disturbing news to Tasha, the limousine slowly pulled off and drove toward the airport.

Once again another friend had crossed him. Now Peter J. Greenberg, was another new name added to his long list of enemies.

*** * * COMING SOON * * ***

BLACK SCARFACE III

THE WRATH OF FACE

DASAINT ENTERTAINMENT ORDER FORM

ORDERING BOOKS

Please visit www.dasaintentertainment.com to place online orders.

You can also fill out this form and sent it to:
DASAINT ENTERTAINMENT
PO BOX 97
BALA CYNWYD, PA 19004

TITLE	PRICE	QTY
BLACK SCARFACE	$15.00	______
BLACK SCARFACE II	$15.00	______
YOUNG RICH & DANGEROUS	$15.00	______
WHAT EVERY WOMAN WANTS	$15.00	______
THE UNDERWORLD	$15.00	______
A ROSE AMONG THORNS	$15.00	______

Make Checks or Money Orders out to: DASAINT ENTERTAINMENT

NAME:____

ADDRESS:_____________________________________

CITY:____

STATE:_____ ZIP:_____

TELEPHONE:___________________________________

EMAIL:_______________________________________

Add $2.50 each book for shipping and handling
($4.95 For Expedited Shipping per item)

WE SHIP TO PRISONS!!!

41197487R00152

Made in the USA
Lexington, KY
03 May 2015